# BAGGAGE

## ALAN MULAK, DONNA SMITH, SUE PASCUCCI

outskirts
press

# About the Authors

Alan Mulak, a retired professional engineer, spends his time blissfully pounding away at the keyboard, living his dream. Mr. Mulak splits his time between South Carolina and Colorado, where he and his wife Ann enjoy their daughters, grandsons, and friends. *Baggage* is his fourth book.. Among his other published books is his best seller, *Reboot*.

Susan Pascucci, a former English teacher from Connecticut, retired to an active adult community in South Carolina where she has kept busy with a wide variety of activities, from water aerobics and yoga to writing groups and book clubs. Although she has printed numerous books for family and friends, *Baggage* is her first published book.

Donna Barnes Smith, a retired educator from Virginia, spends much of her time turning real events into fiction. When she isn't writing, Donna is reading, swimming or walking in her active adult community in South Carolina, near her son, daughter, and granddaughters. *Baggage* is her first published book.

# INTRODUCTION

Two English teachers and an engineer walk into a bar. Actually, since it's the middle of the coronavirus and bars are closed, they meet on zoom. All three are members of Sun City Carolina Lakes' Writers' Guild who discover that the burst of creativity released by enforced isolation was short-lived, and they crave the encouragement that community has long offered writers.

And thus, they begin...

*Fiction is the willing suspension of disbelief*

*—Samuel Coleridge*

# DEDICATION

Alan: I dedicate this book to the memory of my mother, Pauline Mulak, and my mother-in-law, Gertrude Robertie. They both dreamed of travel, but wars, babies, and life got in the way. My hope for them is wherever they may be, they have found three suitcases and are travelling the world over. Who knows, they might even be travelling together!

Donna: I dedicate this book to my daughter Karen Smith Autry, who always listened patiently to my angst over deadlines and finding ideas; to my son David Smith, who actually found three suitcases near a dumpster and inspired the round-robin technique; and, to my late husband Tom, who always encouraged me to write and is pleased that I found something creative to do with all my spare time.

Sue: I dedicate this book to my parents who always encouraged me to expand my horizons - "Give it a try. You never know..."; to my husband Bill, who has been my supportive partner of 56 years; and to my children Robin Pascucci, Dana Dembski, Jill Pierce, and Jim Pascucci, who loved that their mom, even in her senior years, was willing to test new waters.

# ONE

As soon as I spotted them sitting beside the dump-ster, I immediately looked over my shoulder to find their owner. I saw no one, shrugged, then tossed my trash bags over the side and heard them thunk onto piles of other residents' junk. I looked forward to my one day off, reveling in the fact that my apartment was clean for the week and it wasn't even noon.

Before closing my car trunk, I glanced again at the three pieces sitting on their wheels, small-medium-large, almost begging for my attention. Shook my head and scanned the parking lot. Who would abandon three pieces of luggage? Must be a trick or a scam or even a dead body. Suppose there were body parts in there, cut up and bagged into a matching set. I wondered what would happen if I unzipped the big one and found a bloody mess of humanity. Call the police and get ar-rested on the spot?

I slammed the trunk and walked over to the apartment complex office. "Good morning, Crystal. Afternoon, I guess. Just cleaning my place, throwing away some trash in the dumpster. How are you?"

"Thomas, long time no see. Must be your lone day off, huh? Same ol' same ol', you know?"

"Yep, well, uh, do you know anything about those suitcases outside, over by the dumpster? They're just sitting there, but they don't look like trash. They look brand new."

"Nope."

"Do you, uh, wanna come with me while I open them? I mean, don't want to be appearing to steal anything or get in anybody's stuff, but, I mean... ." Oh, God, Crystal was so pretty, but not the sharpest tack in the room. I'd never ask her out, but she always makes me feel so—insecure.

"Sure. Hold on a sec." She pushed a few buttons on the phone, grabbed the office keys and slid out from behind her desk, wearing flip-flops that matched a hot pink mini skirt and a form-fitting tank top.

"Unzip, Sherlock."

"What? Oh, sure. Here goes." I felt so stupid for being scared but grabbed the big one and yanked on the pull-tab. ZZZiiipppp! Nothing, thank the Lord. To my relief, the other two were equally empty, completing a matched set.

"I hereby proclaim you the proud owner of a new set of luggage. Have a nice trip, Thomas!" She wiggled her fingers and flip-flopped her way back to the office. "Ciao!"

Yeah, right, I thought, throwing the bags in my trunk. Slamming the trunk felt good, solid somehow. My hands tingled and my vision blurred for a moment. Little did I know how that moment would change my life forever.

After grabbing lunch at the nearest drive-through, I drove home, wishing I really did have somewhere to go. Satisfied that all the interior pockets of my travel bags were empty, I stretched out for a power nap.

The darkness surprised me when I woke up, reaching for my phone to check the time. No phone, no table lamp, no king-size bed. I sprang up. This was not my room. What the hell? The only familiar items were my new-found bags, three matching pieces, small-medium-large, waiting for me. I stepped onto a bare wood floor and crept two paces to a small window. Morning darkness. I looked out onto a red-tiled roof, three stories from an alley below.

With no other place to sit, I plunked back down on the narrow bed, not even twin-size. Where the hell was I? What did I do yesterday? No alcohol, not even a beer. Maybe this is Crystal's place. "Yeah, right. Who are you kidding?" I didn't mind talking to myself, but I did mind being in a strange place. I stared at the wooden door just inches from the foot of the bed. Panic struck. I'd been kidnapped. Imprisoned. Somehow that luggage was a ploy, a plant, a hoax to capture me and...

"Oh, get a grip, Thomas. Just open the door." It's hard to feign bravery when I'm the only one around, but here goes.

The door pulled open easily, hardly even latched, much less locked. The only noise was my own panting. I stepped into a dark hallway and stared down onto what looked like a small lobby, candlelight flickering from one lone sconce on the wall. Too much. I closed the door, sat back on the bed, then curled into a knot. Worried I'd lost my mind.

Hours must have passed. Sun shone in through my

squinted eyes. I felt over for the rest of my own king mattress, but my arm fell off the side. "Shit! Shit, shit, shit! O.K. What's going on?"

Gather your strength, Thomas. Here goes nothing. Which is exactly what I walked out with—nothing but the clothes on my back and leather sandals on my feet. The hell with the stupid suitcases.

Down the steps, voices bellowed from outside the lobby of this stone-floored place, hotel, whatever. People laughing and wagon wheels clattering over cobblestone streets.

"Leonardo! Leonardo! Ciao!"

I pressed myself against the stone wall. Stone everywhere. Stone and cobblestone and wagon wheels and no English. I combed my fingers through the curly hair on my head, mainly to make sure it was still there. That guy looked like me, the one across the alley. His Grecian nose and average height matched mine.

"Ciao, Thomasino. Come with me. The day is half over, and you promised to work with me today. Today you are my apprentice, right? *Inaction saps the vigor of the mind,* my friend."

He wasn't speaking English, but I could understand him somehow. I said nothing, but what choice did I have? I smiled and followed him across a wide plaza, full of people and what looked like a renaissance bazaar. No one seemed to notice my faded jeans, my t-shirt. Was I really wearing a "You're Killing Me Smalls" shirt? I looked the same age as this Leonardo guy, 32-33 years old, but he strutted around like he owned the streets.

We walked into an enormous studio, like a warehouse, covered with easels and notebooks and drawings and paint. The pungent smell nearly knocked me out, but familiar oil palettes threw me back to my old art class, from back in the day.

"My God!" I shook, staring at what I knew to be the Vitruvian man, a cultural icon by Leonardo da Vinci. From the fifteenth century. This was no joke. But what was it?

"Come, my good friend, my apprentice for the day. You are here for too little time. *Learning is the only thing the mind never exhausts, never fears, and never regrets.* Yes?"

Against my better judgement, I finally spoke, whether he understood me or not. "What am I doing here? Can't you see I don't belong here? I'm, I'm...".

"I know that you have always been interested in my drawing of the Vitruvian Man. What interests you about it, Thomasino?"

"Uh, not sure, really. The, uh, precision, the symmetry?"

"You do belong here, Thomasino. You see exactly what I wanted to portray. I am passionate about the beauty, complexity and symmetry of the human figure. This drawing portrays perfect proportion, my friend. I created a mathematical diagram that is ultimately abstract, yes? You like abstract art, I know. I am familiar with all your paintings you have hung in your apartment."

Dare I disagree with this master, this genius, my childhood idol? I just stared at his rendition of the Roman architect Vitruvius. "Uh, it's so perfect, so exact, how can it be considered abstract," I asked, my meek question coming out in what I assumed was perfect Italian.

"Because the beauty of the abstract is creating something that exists in your mind but does not have a true physical or concrete existence. I think you prefer to create *random* art, so you do not have to plan or make any conscious decision. Is it so hard, Thomasino?

"Look at this human creation. Do you see how the four legs and four arms allow our man to strike sixteen different poses simultaneously? Amazing, is it not? Spread your arms out to your sides, my apprentice. Do you see how the length of your arms from fingertip to fingertip is equal to your height? Isn't that magnificent?"

I stood there in Leonardo da Vinci's studio with my arms outstretched, nodding and wanting more. And the master gave me more, explaining the relationship of all body parts to each other...fingers to palm, palms to foot, and so on. I saw the work and exactness in his drawing and understood the value of creating with precision.

"It can't be happening," I stammered.

He laughed then and pulled up a stool. "Now watch and listen. We only have until the sun goes down. *It's not enough that you believe what you see. You must understand what you see. Life is pretty simple: You do some stuff. Most fails. Some works. You do more of what works.* Please take this notebook and write down as much as you can of what I am doing today. I will dictate. Watch me, then write what I tell you. Call this chapter 'Pyramid of Sight' as I plan to show you the importance of linear perspective."

I wrote and watched for hours, at first silently bemoaning my least favorite part of the only art class I took in school. Order. Structure. Disciplined creativity.

But as I watched and jotted down this master's words, I began to understand the undeniable link between objects and space. Abstract, not random.

At the end of the day, I stumbled back up three narrow flights of stairs and fell into the little bed, those suitcases greeting me with their familiar stance. When I woke up, I reached across the mattress, disappointed to discover more space than I had hoped. Small-medium-large seemed to stare at me, daring me to explore them again.

# Two

I looked around the room, trying to get my bearings. Where was I? *When* was I? What day was it? What year was it? I lurched over to the window, stared out at the familiar landscape below, and breathed a little easier. At least I knew where I was. Nothing changed here. But what about me? Had I changed? Did I carry a bit of Renaissance grandeur? A little Leonardo panache?

I looked in the mirror. Nope, same old boring Thomas. But wait! Maybe there was something a little different. The figure staring back at me looked a bit more self-assured, wiser even. I cocked my head and raised an eyebrow. Could be. Only one way to find out for sure. I opened my door and started down to the lobby, hoping Crystal was still there.

"Hey Crystal," I said as I approached the desk.

She barely looked up at me. "Oh hi, Thomas." Fifteen more minutes and she was out of here.

I took a deep breath. I needed her to really look at me. If she noticed a difference, then it was real. If not, then, like the endings I used to put on my stories for English class, "It was all a dream."

I leaned confidently against the wall, ankles crossed, a look of amused detachment on my face, and channeled my inner Paul Newman.

"So, how's your day been?" Not a great line, but a start.

"Oh, you know, the usual boring stuff. It never changes." She was busy straightening her desk and gathering her things. She still hadn't looked at me.

"Yeah, that's tough, and you know, *inaction saps the vigor of the mind.*" I held my hand in front of me and looked casually at my fingernails.

"What?" That got her attention. She looked at me, puzzled. "What the hell does that mean?" She studied me carefully. "Thomas, what's going on? You look different." She softened and leaned closer to me. "Verrrry different," she purred. "Has something happened? Have I missed something?"

"Well, you know, *everything connects to everything else.*"

"Yeah, I guess. If you say so." She looked unsure. I needed to move fast.

"You know those suitcases I found? Well there's something very special about them." Careful now, Thomas. Don't scare her away. "I was hoping you'd come up and check them out." And maybe, I added to myself, we could do a little time time-travel together.

She laughed brightly. "Now there's a pick-up line I've never heard before, and actually, it sounds kind of inviting, but I'm meeting an old friend for drinks and dinner in about ten minutes."

Sure, the usual brush-off. At least she made up a good excuse. I slumped, feeling the old me taking over.

"But I'll take a rain check," she said as she grabbed keys and phone, flashed me a smile, and flip-flopped out of the building.

I climbed back up to my apartment, determined not to be too discouraged. I wandered into the kitchen, mechanically opened the refrigerator door, stared at the nearly empty shelves, and grabbed one of my diminishing stash of beers. "One of these days I'm really going to have to do some shopping," I muttered. Yes, I do talk to myself now and then. There was a container of leftover mac and cheese that hadn't grown anything green yet; I'd nuke that for dinner later.

Now I just needed to get through the evening. I plunked down onto my couch, took a few good swigs of beer, and decided to take stock of my life.

*Negatives:* work 6 days a week in a bookstore nobody bothers to enter; no social life; no cable TV since Comporium cut it off just because I didn't pay the bill; no friends

*Positives:* not too bad looking, and . . .

Oh shit! I needed another few glugs of beer.

I sat staring into the gathering darkness, letting my familiar cloud of gloom gather around me. Then I saw Leonardo, confidently strolling down the street; heard him saying: *Inaction saps the vigor of the mind.* Do something, Thomas. Positives. Yeah, I have a few. I mean, how many people have had the opportunity to work with Leonardo Da Vinci? He saw something in me.

I recalled the sights and smells of his studio- all the drawings and sketches and half-finished paintings. And the Vitruvian Man – that iconic figure, arms and legs outstretched, that has graced so many textbooks. He made me see it with new eyes. It was right there, under my fingertips! Yeah, I have a few positives.

I wandered over to my bookshelves, filled with

books I regularly brought home from the bookstore, intending to read some day, piled helter-skelter in front of some that go back to college and even high school. I never could get myself to throw out a book, especially not one I had underlined and taken notes in.

I rummaged around until I found *The History of Western Art,* the text from one of my favorite college classes with Dr. Spruance. Each painting he discussed came to life on the screen. I thumbed through until I found the chapter on Leonardo, swelling with pride as I recalled that I had *been* there.

And while I had my nose in this long-neglected section of my bookcase, I found a few old soldiers from my other favorite courses – Philosophy, U. S. History, British Novel. I caught sight of *Great Expectations* and smiled. Now maybe I have some great expectations? Crystal, maybe? She didn't exactly say no. I started thumbing through the book, remembering Pip and Miss Havisham and dear old Joe Gargery. And Pip does eventually get together with Estella, though I hope I don't have to wait that long to make it with Crystal.

Before long, I was beginning to nod off. I got up and stumbled into the bedroom, almost tripping over the suitcases. I plopped down on the bed, wondering whether those three beauties really did have magical powers.

This time when I woke up, it was with a sense of anticipation rather than dread. Had I once again traveled back in time? If so, what period of history was I about to enter? Who would I meet? Or maybe the first time was a fluke and this time I'd be dumped in some nameless time amid nameless people. Or I'd wake up back in my same old room.

I opened my eyes and looked around. The room was sparsely but comfortably furnished in a style we now call Victorian. The three suitcases were sitting there at the foot of the bed challenging me to begin my adventure.

I opened the door, walked down the gas-lit corridor and out onto the street. Before I could even discern where I was, my senses went into high alert: smoke-laden air stung my eyes; fetid odors rising from the street made me gag; I heard a clopping and rumbling coming toward me but failed to jump back in time to avoid a drenching spray from an open sewer as a horse and carriage blew past me. It was almost enough to send me back to my room pleading with the suitcases to take me home.

Almost, but not quite. When I was finally able to clear my vision, the sight took my breath away. The scene before me could have fallen off the pages of the illustrated copy of *A Christmas Carol* that my grandfather read to me every Christmas Eve. I half-expected to see Bob Cratchit dashing into Scrooge's Counting House.

"Thomas! Thomas! Over here!" a voice called to me from across the street. And indeed, it might have been a bewhiskered Bob Cratchit.

I headed across the cobblestones, adjusting my timing to avoid oncoming horses and their drays, and checking my foot placement to sidestep their substantial leavings.

"You handled that almost like a native Londoner," said the dapper gentleman who appeared to be about my age. "I was told I might expect you."

"Wait!" I stammered. "Are you who I think you are?"

He laughed good-naturedly. "I guess that all depends."

"Charles . . . um . . . Charles Dickens?"

He laughed again and nodded. "Come now. I have a job I need you to do."

"Wait! What could I possibly help you do? Bottom line, I'm pretty useless."

"*No one is useless in this world who lightens the burden of another.* Come along now."

He led me into a spacious office. Scattered on top of his expansive desk were several small pieces of paper, and leaning against the wall was a long wide board.

"Have you ever wanted to do any writing Thomas? Serious writing, I mean?" he asked as he rummaged through the papers on his desk.

I was shocked. I had never told anyone of my foolish dream of some day writing a bestselling novel. "Yeah, a little, I guess," I murmured. "But I don't know how to go about it or even what to write. I'm not smart enough to think up all that stuff."

"As far as what to write, *a loving heart is the truest wisdom.* And as far as how to do it, that's what you are about to help me with. As you know, I write my stories in segments, which are published periodically in magazines. Now the problem is that generally even I am not sure where the story is going until I start writing. I let the characters tell me where they need to go. For the most part I am, so to speak, 'flying by the seat of my pants.' But as you can imagine that method generates a bit of anxiety, since I can't be assured that my characters are always on speaking terms with me, and my publisher won't tolerate any such excuses.

"Now this next book that I am writing is called *The Personal History, Adventures, Experience and Observation of David Copperfield the Younger of Blunderstone Rookery (Which He Never Meant to Publish on Any Account).*"

I couldn't help myself. "With all due respect, you might consider calling it just *David Copperfield*. Easier for people to remember, especially school kids."

He greeted my suggestion with a puzzled look and then pushed it aside. "Yes, well anyway, this time I have plotted out the whole story in advance and written each major event on a slip of paper. Then I am going to put it over there on what I am calling a storyboard. That's where you come in. The glue pot is here. I'll hand you the paper and tell you where I think it should go. If you have any suggestions, of course, I'll be happy to entertain them."

The day passed quickly, the two of us working together like a well-oiled machine. I did make one small contribution. Charles had initially named the slimy, twisted clerk who was to be the bane of David's existence, Aaron Hemp. I suggested that Uriah Heep might better convey his character, for which he thanked me profusely.

Before I knew it, it was time for me to leave. My face must have reflected my sadness. What an amazing thing it had been to work under the tutelage of the great Charles Dickens. A tear slipped down my cheek and I hastily wiped it away. He smiled and clapped his hand on my shoulder. "Ah Thomas. *We need never be ashamed of our tears.*"

I just nodded, hesitant to trust my voice.

"Indeed, this has been a most delightful day and I will miss you. But remember, *the pain of parting is nothing to the joy of meeting again.*"

I practically floated back to my room in the inn, unaware of the smoke and smells and chaos of mid-nineteenth-century London. I had met Charles Dickens! And though I can't say I was crazy about *David Copperfield* when I had to read it in ninth grade, I was certainly going to gobble it up as soon as I got back home.

I entered my room, gave the suitcases a loving pat, lay down on the bed and closed my eyes, eager to get back home and try out the new me.

# THREE

"Good morning, Crystal," I said as I approached the desk the following morning.

"Hey Thomas, where you off to?"

"Work."

"You're always working! You probably already told me, but I forgot. Where is it you work?"

"*The BookWorm - New and Used Books*. It's a hole in the wall off Main Street, across from the post office."

"Books? What kind of books?"

I shrugged. "All kinds. Typical bookstore stuff. We get in all genres and authors." I paused, then was struck with an idea. "Do you have a favorite writer? I could keep an eye out and maybe snag a first edition for you."

"No, not really. I'm not into reading books. I like magazines with lots of pictures." She studied her nails, clearly unhappy with the paint job. "What do you do there?"

"Mostly, just babysit the shop. These days, the book business is slow. But every now and then, Horace, he's the owner, will buy someone's personal library at an estate sale, and sometimes, we'll discover a rare edition, and if it's in mint condition, then life gets exciting."

"Sounds...well, I'll have to take your word for it." She shrugged, now taking a file to the nail on her forefinger. "Work is work."

I laughed and exhaled a breath of resignation. "You got that right. And by the way, how was your dinner last night?"

She looked up and smiled. "Oh that. It was, you know, just kind of, well, boring."

It was my turn to smile. "I'll bet it's because you were thinking about how you wished you were there with me." Oh shit! I can't believe I just said that. Nice going moron.

Crystal blinked, mouth agape. "Well actually, you're right."

"I am?"

She sensuously brushed a stray hair off her forehead. "I'm taking today and tonight off to help my mom move to her new apartment, but tomorrow night, I'm free. Maybe I could cash in that rain check? I'm not much of a gourmet cook but can open a bottle of wine with the best. Dinner at my place?"

My mouth was dry. "Sounds wonderful."

The room temperature climbed as Crystal stared at me as I stared at her. Finally, she stood and picked up her car keys.

"I've gotta go," she said. "Mom's waiting. Can't wait to tomorrow eve." Then she actually blushed – perhaps coyly, perhaps not. "I can't believe I just said that."

"Just remember," I said. *"The pain of parting is nothing to the joy of meeting again."*

Horace was already there when I arrived to open the shop. This was most unusual. I knew something was up. As I stepped through the door, the little copper bell hanging above the door dinged my arrival.

"Mornin' Horace," I announced. "This is a surprise. You're here early."

"Well Thomas," he replied, hands on hips in obvious disgust. "I had some books delivered, and the delivery gorillas were only available at this ungodly hour. But alas, I'm afraid I've wasted my money on this lot." He pointed to seven cardboard boxes, all full to the brim with hardcover books.

Horace was the shop owner and overall, a good boss. Generally, I would not see nor hear from him for weeks at a time, which worked out well for us both. If I had to guess at his age, I'd say about fifty. A few years back, he had purchased the failing business from a trio of successful authors who wanted to spend the rest of their days writing a series of mystery novels from the Caribbean. Horace decided to keep the shop name, *The BookWorm* – something about name recognition – and try to breathe new life into a dying trade. So far, it was not happening. He said the shop had always been a bookstore going way back to the sixties when it was owned by some hippies.

A likeable fellow, Horace described himself as "extra-large with two sugars." Unlike me, there was nothing about him that blended into the background. Take his attire for example. Today, he wore a flaming red silk shirt which covered his expansive bulk like a tent. He had flowing, swept back, dyed blond hair with a touch a lime green around the temples. He wore many rings and a gold chain held his reading glasses, which were now dangling down to his chest. And also, he did not believe in physical labor – that's why he hired me. Yet he paid me well and allowed me to run the shop the way I wanted.

Horace was a generous man. When, on the occasion he would show up at lunch time, he always arrived with two bags of whatever the Cuban Sandwich shop next door was making as their daily special, and two bottles of chilled Perrier to wash it all down.

He spoke of travels and vacations to far-off exotic places but to my knowledge, they were just fantasies as he never seemed to take any extended time off.

In fact, I am not sure where he goes or what he does when he leaves the shop. We enjoy a 'don't ask, don't tell' relationship and actually, are quite relaxed with each other.

In spite of my best efforts to organize, the shop was a reflection of Horace, filled beyond capacity. There were numerous stacks of books that I waged war with, waiting for shelf space to be made available. Horace would bring them in, I would try to find a place to store them. It was just like the ocean tides.

And now he had done it again; this time with seven over-stuffed boxes. These new additions had been unceremoniously dropped in the middle of the ever-shrinking open floor space, and now, there was no place to go. It was way too claustrophobic. Rolling up my sleeves, I got busy. First the SALE table was rolled out onto the sidewalk, then I shoved the boxes over against the stacks, opening more space. Now, if a customer was to drop in, they would at least have room to move.

Next, I flipped the CLOSED sign over, turned on the lights, and finally, busied myself with the vital process of making a pot of freshly ground coffee.

Horace was slipshod about many things, but not coffee. We drank only ridiculously expensive Ethiopian dark beans, grinding each batch to a fine consistency, and then pouring in filtered, bottled spring water. Any deviation from this exacting procedure was cause for immediate dismissal.

And then there was the cat, Meow. Technically, the cat belonged to Horace but, in actuality it owned the shop. In the morning, it would sit in the sun in the front window and watch my every move. We had one of those relationships that can be described as mutual tolerance. Simply put; we stayed clear of each other. When Horace was not in the shop – which was most of the time - Meow would disappear somewhere among the stacks, exactly where, I do not know.

"Well, Horace," I said, sweeping the floor with an old-fashioned corn-fiber broom, pushing the tracked-in detritus out the opened door, raising clouds of dust in the process, "as far as wasting your money goes, you never know. All it takes is one rare gem."

He walked over to the coffee pot, poured two mugs, and brought me one. "Stop that," he said, handing me my coffee and taking the broom from my hand. "You're making me all sweaty just watching you."

We chatted about the boxes of new acquisitions and since most of the books were book club editions, they would go directly into the SALE cart and be sold for shortchange. Anything of potential value would be stacked – sigh – and evaluated on a book-by-book basis.

Then he was gone, the bell above the door signaling his departure.

Sorting through and categorizing the books was enjoyable. I find it exciting. As expected, most were of little value and went straight out to the sidewalk. There were many books on sports, some of which were first editions in great shape. And there was also a stack of history books, some of value. But one book in particular caught my attention. It was entitled *Landscape Turned Red: The Battle of Antietam* by Stephen Sears. I am not a history buff by a long shot; in fact I failed U.S. History in college, but this volume was curious.

I flipped through the book and took note of all the annotations and yellow highlighting. Someone had studied the pages as one would a textbook. Then I looked it up online and the reviews were outstanding. It was – is – considered to be the definitive work on the subject.

Interesting.

I put it aside.

As always, Horace returned with lunch consisting of cooked ham, roast pork, melted swiss, fresh Cuban roll, six dill pickles, iced Perrier with a slice of lime. We ate, he departed, and then I opened the book on the counter and began to read. The prologue was entitled "The Last Best Hope," and as it turned out, was true. I was sucked into the book and the pages flipped by, relating the horrifying story of wasted American lives. All I could think of was those young men whose lives had been squandered by incompetent leadership.

It was well after five PM when I forced myself to close the book, flip over the OPEN sign, wheel the SALE cart back inside, turn off the lights, and go home.

As I came into my apartment, I tossed the book onto my unmade bed and began flipping through the mail. It was then I absentmindedly tripped over the suitcases, small – medium – large, which had been pushed against the wall. Catching myself, I put my hand down upon the large suitcase to keep from falling. In doing so, I felt the now familiar tingling in my hands, and a slight blurring of my vision. But then it passed.

Supper was Cuban Shrimp Stew – leftover from lunch earlier in the week – and without further delay, I got right back into the book. Sometime before midnight I finished it, turned off the light, and fell asleep.

I lay in the morning darkness, eyes closed, aware of the sounds that seemed to be coming from all directions. Men's voices, horses neighing, the tramp of many feet. It smelled strongly of fresh coffee, wood smoke, and horse shit. I reached out to my left and my hand touched the wall, but the wall yielded slightly to my touch, and it felt like canvas. Slowly, I sat up and let my eyes adjust to the low light. Where was I?

Then the flap was pulled open, allowing the onset of daybreak to paint my space with yellow tones. A man in a blue uniform stood in the doorway. I blinked away the night and looked all around – I was in a tent! *What the...?*

"The general will see you now," the man said.

I swung my feet off the cot and stood, rapping my head on a kerosene lantern hanging from the roof of the tent, then followed the man outside.

In every direction, men in blue uniforms sat around campfires with smoke rising unsteadily upward. White clouds of morning mist lay in the low areas of the field, but even as I watched, were disappearing from the first probing rays of the rising sun. Horses, many horses, grazed on dew-dappled meadow grass. Cannons, lined hub to hub, stood ready for action. Tents filled the open spaces, wagons parked nearby.

The man turned to me. "The general is waiting."

"Excuse me," I said, trying to flatten my bed-headed hair. "What is all this? Where am I? And who are you?"

"I'm Lieutenant Becket, General McClelland's adjutant. You are looking at part of the First Corps. This is part of Reynold's Division. And we're just East of Sharpsburg, Maryland."

"And today's date?"

The Lieutenant shot me a quizzical look. "It's September 16."

"And the year?"

He cocked his head. "The *year?* Why it's 1862." It was clear he had some questions, but he kept them to himself.

We strode through the dripping, knee-high grass – soaking our feet in the process – until we came to a farmhouse, which by all appearances, had been requisitioned by the army for temporary headquarters. An American flag was draped across one porch railing while the banner designating the Army of the Potomac covered the other. Armed men snapped to attention, their bayonets glistening in the sunlight, as we mounted the wooden steps.

The Lieutenant held open the door for me. "Go ahead in and take a seat."

I did.

A small man, perfectly coiffed, smartly dressed in a crisp Major General's uniform paced slowly in front of a seated group of Union Generals and their staffs. He exuded the air of a man in charge, with supreme confidence. The Major General kept one hand in his breast coat – just like his hero, Napoleon – and gesticulated with a riding crop in his other. The wall behind him was covered with a huge battle map.

"In review," he said, "General Franklin, you hit their right flank at 7am. I want all artillery firing at 6:30 sharp, to clear your way. General Porter, you hold in the center, and General Burnside, you hold on the left. Generals Porter and Burnside, I want you to demonstrate when Franklin goes in. Make Lee think you are attacking as well. Any questions?"

The room cleared and the Major General approached. I stood.

"I'm Major General McClelland. Are you Thomas?"

"I am."

"I've been expecting you. Follow me."

We marched across the room, entered a back office, and he took a seat behind the desk.

"Close the door," he commanded.

Then he melted. First, he unbuttoned the top button to his tunic, then put his face in his hands.

I looked longingly at the nearby coffee pot. Without asking, while his face was still buried, I helped myself and sipped the vile brew, leaning against the wall.

"My God, my God," he sobbed. "What will become of me? So many men will die. They look to me as their leader, their father, and I am doing all I can. Lincoln has it in for me. He wants me to fail. They all do."

*Bravery is the capacity to perform properly even when scared half to death.* I was scared to death, but if da Vinci and Dickens had faith in me, maybe I had some value after all.

"General," I said. "I think I can help."

He slowly pulled his face from his hands and stared at me, blinking away his tears.

"First," I began tentatively, "Lincoln is not out to get you. He is desperate for a victory. Next," I put down my tin coffee cup and began pacing back and forth in front of his desk. Finding courage that surprised even myself, I was warming to my topic. "Your plan will most assuredly fail. History will remember you as the general that missed an opportunity to win the war, and you missed it because you refused to act." Shit, I hope I'm not going too far. I looked at his face. He was still listening. I drew closer and rested my hands on his desk, face to face. "Tomorrow General, put in all your men. Send in Porter and Burnside at 7 am with Franklin. Lee only has one-third the soldiers you do, and his back is against a flooded river. He can't retreat! You can win the war tomorrow! You will then be the greatest general ever. If you do, you will beat Lincoln in the next election. All your dreams will come true!"

"But so many will die!" He moaned.

"And if you don't do as I suggest, the war will drag on for three more years and half a million men will die. They don't have to. You can do it!"

More inconsolable whining.

"General." I leaned in close. "There was a reason you sent for me. It's because I know what's going to happen, and I can advise you on a way to reduce the slaughter. You have the means at your fingertips. You can change the course of history. Yes, men will die tomorrow, but your way, your plan, is a piecemeal approach and your men, the ones who idolize you as their savior, they will be butchered."

"No, no, no." He went back to sobbing, face in hands.

I stood and stared down at the pathetic man. Patton once said, *A true soldier does not admit defeat before the battle.* This man was already defeated. History was right about him. There was nothing I could do. I turned and left his office.

As I strolled back toward my tent, my thoughts were aswirl. I paused and took in the spectacle all around: blue troops were striking their tents. The army was getting ready to spring into action. Soldiers were moving with a purpose. I slowly shook my head. Quietly, I said aloud, "Why am I here?"

"Thomas?"

I spun around. A bearded man with wire-rimmed glasses, about my size, was standing behind me. He wore a stained surgeon's apron and an infantry cap. As he removed his gloves, he held me in his gaze. Smiling, he asked, "You're Thomas, right?"

I nodded. "Yep. And you are?"

He extended his hand. "John Woodworth. Mind if I walk with you?"

"Be my guest."

We fell into step through the tall grass. The morning dew had evaporated in the hot August sun. The fog which had hugged the ground earlier had been replaced with a layer of dust and pollen.

My companion began, "Forgive me for eavesdropping but I overheard every word of your meeting with the commanding general."

Alarmed, I stopped and looked at Woodworth. "You did?"

"I was standing outside the door, waiting to get an authorization signed." He nodded in the direction of the general's headquarters. "The walls are paper-thin. I couldn't help but listen." He shrugged. "No worries. Your secrets are safe with me."

A horse-drawn carriage, artillery piece attached, came rumbling by. He pointed towards my tent which stood all the way across the meadow. "Let's get a move on before we get run down."

As we strode, my companion shot a glance my way. "You have to understand, I'm just a surgeon and know little about warfare and strategy but from what I heard, your argument sounded like good advice."

I nodded.

"And," he continued, "the idea of winning the war and going home sounds pretty damn square."

Again, I nodded.

We were nearly at my tent when he touched my arm and we stopped, looking at each other. "But then I heard you say '...*There was a reason you sent for me. It's because I know what's going to happen...*'."

My heart was pounding.

Woodworth held up his hand. "You're not in danger. I'm not a spy or anything like that. It's just that, well, it was a curious thing to say."

I licked my lips and looked all around to make sure we were far away from possible listeners. "It's like this," I began. "It's a really long story and I sure as hell don't understand but I'm...I'm...I'm a time traveler." I paused. Woodworth was hanging on my every word. "I'm from the future. And for some reason, I get sent to all sorts of places."

He cocked his head. "Quite a tale. Quite a tale." He

nodded a few times, clearly digesting what I'd just told him. "So, let's say you're not crazy and do, in fact, get sent to different times and places. Why?"

"Why? Beats the shit out of me. But I think I'm supposed to learn something when I travel. I really don't know."

Woodworth removed his glasses and began cleaning them on a tattered red handkerchief. "Well, again, let's say that's true. What did you learn here in Sharpsburg, Maryland, on the eve of a big battle?"

I folded my arms and watched the First Division slinging their packs and marching away. "I really don't know."

He stood next to me, watching all the blue troops moving. Many of them, moving towards death.

"Maybe," he said, replacing his glasses. "Maybe you're supposed to learn that you can't change history, no matter how hard you try or how right you are or how much you want to."

I stared at him. "You think so?"

He shrugged and smiled. "Not a bad lesson for a time traveler to learn but then again, I'm just a surgeon. How am I supposed to know?"

A squad of cavalry thundered by.

"Incidentally," he said. "Does my name ring a bell with you?"

I blinked a few times. "John Woodworth? Hmm. Can't say it does. Why do you ask?"

It was his turn to surreptitiously look all around. He leaned close to me and in hardly more than a whisper, said, "When this war is over, the President is going to create a new governmental position. He's going to name it Surgeon General. And he's going to appoint me to be the first Surgeon General of the United States."

He smiled again, shook my hand, and walked off. Stunned, I stood there for a long, long time.

The next evening, I knocked on Crystal's door. From inside, I could hear booming music thumping away. I knocked again, louder. Then the door swung open and there she was, wearing jeans and some sort of pink spandex top – both of which about two sizes too small. It was pretty clear that was *all* she wore. The acrid odor of burning cardboard filled my nostrils.

"Come in," she said. "Please forgive the smell. I tried to cook one of those gourmet meals you pick up in the frozen food aisle, but it caught fire in the oven."

I looked around. The windows were open wide, and several candles were flickering. In the kitchen, the oven door was open and therein was the charred remains of a party-sized Stouffer's baked ziti. I blinked away the smoke. "I think you're supposed to take it out of the box before baking."

"Yeah," she said," I think you're right." She shrugged and dismissed the mess with the wave of her hand. "First time for everything. Oh well. So, the main course tonight will be a Sal's pizza with s'hrooms, onions, and anchovies. It should be arriving any minute."

Just for the record, I hate anchovies. But no matter.

By the time we plowed through the pizza – I ate around those salty little fish - and emptied two bottles of wine, the air had cleared, and the lights were dimmed.

We moved to the sofa. Now, in retrospect, and I am certainly no expert at such things, but I believe it is always a bad sign when someone's space looks better in candlelight – the fewer candles, the better. But then again, when I am in lust and the promise of sex is looming, all but the vital senses tend to blur, so it really did not matter.

More wine, cuddling and caressing, and more wine. Time for the next step. Crystal excused herself to go powder her nose and returned wearing a silk kimono, which was on the floor in no time.

As stated earlier, I am no expert at these things but Crystal's nude body had been surgically enhanced to a cartoonish extent. I appreciate the effort I suppose, but she looked more like an undressed female manikin than a natural woman. And I know enough about myself to believe I am not the kind of guy who makes women howl. Her passionate yodeling was so jarring and startling that I thought she was in some sort of dire distress. What the hell did the neighbors think?

# Four

I left Crystal feeling empty. Hungry, yes, but something else, too. The more eager she seemed to please me, the less appealing she became. She couldn't cook, dressed like a teenager, and had no interest in traveling. "Who am I kidding. I could be talking about myself."

And yet.

Climbing the stairs to my own apartment made me wonder where I was really going. She had said, "Same ol', same ol'," but there had to be more. What has happened to me? I used to have dreams, aspirations, career goal, interests. I've quit college, work six days a week in a dead-end job, and eat fast food every chance I get. Is this really all there is?

And there they were. Small-medium-large. Sitting at the foot of my bed as if waiting for me to touch them. Instead, I took a hot shower, toweled off and sat on the end of the bed. "Life is short and then you die." That's what Dad always said. He meant get off your ass and make something of yourself. "Tomorrow I'll cook myself a decent meal."

I dared to tap the handle of the nearest suitcase, shrugged and stretched out for the night.

"Boeuf Bourguignon, Quiche Lorraine, Cheese Souffle, Vichyssoise. Which should we try first, Thomas?"

That voice. Where had I heard that voice before? High-pitched, almost comical, but sincere? Turning around, I had to look up to see the lady in front of me. She was a good six inches taller than I and looked a bit like a man in drag. Frumpy. Disheveled. But the apron and her smile caught me off guard. "What?"

"Which shall we try first? I want you to choose."

Am I really standing in a commercial kitchen in front of Julia Child? I shook my head and looked out the window. Clearly, I was not in North Carolina anymore. "I'm sorry, what?"

"I've come back to the school to teach you for the day," she trilled. "Grab an apron and stop gawking. We only have eight hours. Decide, Thomas."

"Uh, Boeuf Bourguignon, I guess. But I can't do this. I've never—"

"Of course you can. *I was thirty-two when I started cooking; up until then, I just ate.* Now grab those onions and watch how I slice them."

Once again, I decided the best path to take was one of silent obedience. I didn't want to appear inept. She would discover that soon enough.

"You know, Thomas, *it's hard to imagine a civilization without onions,* don't you think?" She threw the slices in a large skillet, dropping a few pieces on the floor, not batting an eye. "Grab that bottle of wine, now, and pour a little as I stir."

I tilted out a few drops and the pan sizzled.

"Oh, now I see why you've come to me. You are afraid of making a mistake. Afraid you'll mess something up.

Pour a good dollop in there. You'll get the feel of it. Smell that?"

The aroma made my mouth water. I was quickly working up an appetite.

Her infectious laugh encouraged me. "*I enjoy cooking with wine. Sometimes I even put it in the food.* Lighten up. Have fun, Thomas. After this course, we'll take a stroll outside. I need to buy some butter for our next recipe, and you need to inhale Paris in the springtime. It will help you breathe a new life."

I looked over my shoulder at the door we just exited and saw *LE CORDON BLEU* labeling the arched entrance. Cars passing us along Quai Andre Citroen affirmed that I really was in Paris. Our reflections in the shop windows presented a comic contrast. I saw myself tagging behind a middle-aged woman wearing a bright green polka-dot dress and carrying an oversized purse. My image in khaki shorts and long-sleeved shirt conjured up a schoolboy, sans striped tie, hurrying after her. The April breeze ruffled our curly-haired heads and gave me a spring in my step.

Strolling with Julia Child was no walk in the park. I had to trip double time to keep up with her long legs. She talked as we walked, explaining that she first came to Paris during World War II and couldn't cook a lick. She had met her husband when they both worked for the OSS, precursor to the CIA.

"You were a spy?" I had to ask.

"I've been lots of things, Thomas. *Life itself is the proper binge.* I can see the eagerness in your eyes. You want to explore, but you are afraid." We stopped in front of a small grocery store, quaintly named La Petite Epicerie. "This is where I purchase my butter whenever

I come to Paris. Go in and ask for two pounds. If you're lucky, Chantelle will wait on you."

Reluctantly, I opened the door, prepared to make a total fool of myself fumbling with tenth-grade French. I stood speechless in front of the counter, looking at the most gorgeous girl I had ever seen.

I think she sang, "Bonjour. Comment vas-tu?" Her sparkling blue eyes mesmerized me and I stood frozen, speechless. When I could finally clear my throat, my whispered words came out perfectly, "Le beurre, s'il vous plait," and the smile on Chantelle's face lit up the room. I could get used to this dream transport or whatever it was. I ran my hands through my hair and looked away. Chantelle's statuesque demeanor and ravishing blonde hair convinced me she must be a model in real time. Julia stood outside smiling and watched me gawk.

As we walked back to the kitchen for my next lesson, Julia chided me for my timid approach with the girl. *"Just speak very loudly and quickly, and state your position with utter conviction, as the French do, and you will have a marvelous time,"* she encouraged me.

The remainder of my day with Julia satisfied my appetite and I hoped I could stretch the allotted eight hours into another day, or two. At Julia's direction, I wandered into the hotel lobby across the street and the bellman handed me a key. I found my room on the twelfth floor overlooking the banks of the River Seine. I avoided touching small-medium-large that greeted me inside the suite. Maybe I could see Chantelle again. Exhausted, I lay across the massive bed, closed my eyes and hoped for the best.

# FIVE

When I woke once again in my own bed, I was disappointed . . . sad . . . empty . . . I searched for the right word to express my mood. The bustle and excitement of Paris, the smell of onions, the sizzle of wine pouring into the pan, and the squeaky voice of Julia Child urging me to try my wings – all that sensory excitement was swallowed up by my boring little apartment.

I lay still for a while, mourning my loss. This was a new feeling. Before, when I came back from my suitcase adventures, I felt buoyed up, eager to try out what I had learned. Then I heard Julia saying to me, *Life itself is the proper binge.* I needed to take charge of my life – binge a little. That was it! I didn't have to be in Paris to spice up my life. I could make my own boeuf bourguignon.

I had a zip in my step and a purpose in my walk as I headed out to shop for the needed ingredients. I was so focused that I didn't even notice Crystal.

"Hey Thomas," she called out. "You look pretty perky this morning." She stepped out from behind the desk and stood tantalizingly close to me. "Could it maybe have something to do with last night?" she cooed. A couple of days ago I would have peed my pants to have her that close, but today, I felt vaguely bland.

She must have sensed my reluctance, because she started fiddling with a button on my shirt, and in her most sultry tone said, "Surely you haven't forgotten last night."

No, I definitely hadn't, and although the evening overall left me feeling vaguely unsatisfied, there *was* some pretty amazing stuff going on. A significant part of my body responded to that memory in a way that made me temporarily forget my plans.

"So, I was thinking," she whimpered, sliding her hand further up my chest, "maybe tonight we could try your place. A little wine, a little nibble..." She licked her lips slowly.

"Good idea," I squeaked.

She stepped back, "So, your place at 8 tonight. By the way, where are you headed now?"

I snapped back to attention. "I'm going out to do some shopping. I'll make you a meal that'll knock your socks off." I envisioned Crystal watching in awe as I pulled some of my new Julia Child moves and produced a boeuf bourguignon that she would remember forever.

When she walked in at a little before 8, I was busy frying onions. She wrinkled up her nose as she entered the kitchen.

"What the heck are you cooking?"

"Just fixing some onions. *It's hard to imagine a civilization without onions, wouldn't you agree?*"

"Uh, yeah, I guess so." She didn't seem at all impressed.

"If you want to help, you can pour a dollop of wine," I said handing her the bottle of Sauvignon Blanc I had just purchased. *"I enjoy cooking with wine. Sometimes I even put it in the food."*

"Yeah, if you say so. If you can just pull yourself away from the stove long enough to pour me a glass of wine that I can actually drink, I'll go sit down until you've finished playing."

This was definitely not the response I had envisioned.

The rest of the evening didn't go much better. My boeuf bourguignon was spectacular – almost as good as Julia's – but all Crystal said was, "Stew? I hate stew! I thought you said you were making something special." Her response to my elegant flan was, "You know, you can get pudding in those little cups in the grocery store. It's a lot less trouble."

And although my performance in the kitchen was superb, unfortunately my performance in other areas, deflated by her chilling response, left much to be desired. Crystal left without so much as a good night.

I started cleaning up the mess in the kitchen, but I gave up and came in and plunked down on the couch. I thought of Chantelle, the "butter girl" – her smile, her ravishing blonde hair. She would have cooed, "Mon Cherie, ton boeuf bourguignonne, c'est fantastique!" Not "Stew? I hate stew."

I wanted to forget the whole evening, to wash the taste of failure out of my mouth with something positive – maybe a new adventure. So I lay down on my bed, hoping to be transported to someplace exciting. I tossed and turned for a while before finally falling asleep.

When I woke, I put off opening my eyes, savoring the anticipation. When I finally did open them, I was shocked. I was still in my own bed, in my own room, with my clock registering 7:10, time to get up and go to work. The suitcases were still there, taunting me. Had they lost their magic?

The next night was the same. I was thoroughly dejected. To perk myself up, though, instead of stopping for fast food after work, I went to Whole Foods, bought some fresh ingredients, and treated myself to a chicken cordon-bleu. It was nearly midnight when I finished, but I didn't care. The rest of the week continued along the same way – each day with excited planning, each evening a new dish. Then I lay down to bed with hope, but with decreasing expectations.

Crystal and I passed each other with barely a muffled "hi," but I was fine. I must admit, however, that by the end of the week, I was getting a little worn out. This cooking gig was a lot more work than Julia made it seem. So this time, I picked up a burger and some fries and sat back with a beer to watch the Panthers get pummeled again.

Not far into the first half, I realized that even the Panthers weren't enough to perk me up. I couldn't stop thinking about Chantelle – foolish, of course, since there wasn't a chance we would ever meet again. Still . . .

I picked up a blank piece of paper and started doodling. At one time, I had managed to do some fairly decent drawings, in another lifetime. But a little Leonardo must have rubbed off on me, because her face started to take shape before my eyes. I wasn't going to win any prizes or anything, but it was passable – and what's more, it was fun! I had drawn my heroine; now maybe I could bring her to life in a story that had long been rattling around in my head.

So I started writing – just phrases and ideas at first; then whole sentences started pouring out. I envisioned Charles standing over my shoulder urging me on.

After about a half hour, I stopped writing and eagerly started reading what I had written. Bad move! It was going to take more than a day with Charles Dickens to make a writer out of me. What could I write about that could even begin to interest anyone? My life was pretty pathetic and ordinary – no back alleys of a rough and tumble city, no skeletons in the closet, no adventures on the high seas or hijacked airplanes. I'd never even traveled out of North Carolina. Even after helping Dickens, I had no idea where stories came from. But for some reason, I still really wanted to try my hand at writing.

I crumpled up the paper and tried to shoot it across the room and into the wastepaper basket. I missed.

I have no idea how long I sat there, caught in the neverland between success and failure. But I wasn't going to let everything that had happened recently bring me back to the Old Thomas. I left him at the dumpster when I picked up the suitcases. All those places I'd been and people I'd met – Nope! I wasn't going back. I heard Leonardo: *You do some stuff. Most fails. Some works. You do more of what works.* Boeuf bourguignonne, flan, a passable sketch of a beautiful woman, a very rough first draft. Yup, some stuff works. I just needed to hang onto that.

On that note, I decided to retire for the night. As I

walked into the bedroom, I stopped in front of small-medium-large, gave them a grateful pat, and felt a tingling in my hands. Then I lay down, hoping that maybe the suitcases would work their magic once again. But if they didn't, I had a store of memories that should last me a good long time.

I must have nodded off because when I woke up, I knew the suitcases had indeed done their job. Where was I? I lay in the dark, listening, trying to guess.

The sounds of hearty laughter, song, and muffled voices piqued my interest. I made my way through the small dark room, down the dimly lit hall, and into a tavern filled with boisterous men. The free-flowing beer, raunchy songs, and loud conversation far out-did any frat party I had ever been to. As my eyes gradually adjusted to the hazy room, I saw one group sitting in a corner, gathered around a man who seemed to be holding their attention.

He caught sight of me and called, "Thomas! Thomas! Over here!"

I pushed my way through the crowd and he stood before me.

"Come, have a seat. We're just about to begin. But wait. I forget myself. My friend here is drinkless." He tossed a coin to one of the men nearest the bar. "Would you mind doing the honors?"

"Aye mate," he responded. "But wait . . . "

"Don't worry. We'll not start without you."

Where was I? Who were these people? Should I ask

and feel stupid? Or maybe just wait and see if I could piece it together.

"Conrad," the man called from the bar, "you ready for another one yet?"

Conrad . . . Conrad. I raced through my brain. I turned and looked out the window. There, at the dock not far away was a triple-masted sailing ship, the kind popular in the late 1800's . Things started falling into place. These were clearly sailors, either just arrived in port or about to set sail.

The man came back carrying three drinks. "Now, can we get started?" he asked as he set them down.

Conrad laughed. "Billy Boy here is one of my biggest fans."

"Righto, mate. All those long hours we're out there, nothin' but water for days on end, and Conrad helps us pass the time with his stories."

Aha! Sea ... stories . . .Conrad. I was sitting in a pub listening to the great story-teller Joseph Conrad telling tales to his mates. Now I really wished I had paid better attention in high school English when we were reading *Heart of Darkness*.

Conrad continued, "As I was saying, the white man was about to sail up the river to meet his Malayan friend and his wife, who lived alone in a house on a lagoon." A hush came over the crowd around him.

"Now, instead of *me* describing this river in the Malayan jungle, I'm going to ask you all to give my buddy an idea of what it looks like."

There was a chorus of groans. "C'mon, Conrad. We can't do it like you do," they muttered.

"No, no," he persisted. "We need to give Thomas here a little idea of the world we get to see. Anybody?"

"I'll try," said Billy. "See it's like this. When you get into that jungle, the trees and vines, they start closing in on you and it gets dark – like eerie dark and quiet dark. You know there are critters out there still, watching, but there's no sound, no sound at all. It's something you don't forget."

"Not bad, not bad, mate," Conrad said. "Not bad at all. Pretty soon you'll be taking over for me."

"Uh, uh. Not a chance," grumbled the others.

"Thomas, how about you. Give it a go."

I protested. Secretly, I wanted to give it a shot. After all, I had been doing a little bit of writing and it wasn't all *that* bad. But no, I didn't know these people. Surely they, like everybody else all my life, would just laugh at my foolish attempts. I shook my head and pulled back.

"Come, come, Thomas. *Facing it, always facing it, that's the way to get through. Face it,*" Conrad urged.

Okay. That sounded remarkably like the advice Julia had given me. I'd give it a try. I hadn't been in any exotic far-away jungle, but I had gotten lost in a Florida swamp once – something I'll never forget.

I began. "As we rounded a bend and the river narrowed, the trees closed in overhead and the banks grew so close we could almost touch them with our paddles. We stopped paddling and listened. There was nothing – no sound, no movement – and yet, everything seemed alive. Alive, but unmoving."

I sat back, pleased that I had had the courage to try something like that in front of all these strangers. Maybe Conrad had the right idea. I needed to just *face it.*

"I think I may have some competition here," Conrad said.

"He's not bad, but c'mon, Conrad. We want to hear the master."

"Yeah, get on with it," they grumbled all at once. They had had enough with the amateurs.

Conrad leaned forward, his face half-lit by the lantern on the table, and began:

*The forest, somber and dull, stood motionless and silent on each side of the broad stream. In the stillness of the air, every tree, every leaf, every bough, every tendril of creeper and every petal of minute blossom seemed to have been bewitched into an immobility perfect and final. . .*

He continued, and it seemed as if the tavern had absorbed the stillness from his words, and people hushed. Some wandered over and stood on the edges of Conrad's little group. Others sat respectfully, almost as if they had suddenly found themselves in a church. By the time Conrad had finished his tale of friendship and betrayal and loss, and he left Arsat *still looking through the great light of a cloudless day into the hopeless darkness of the world,* you could hear the waves lapping on the ship outside and the distant voices of people passing by. A few men casually scratched their cheek or looked down into their beer. No doubt about it, Conrad was a master.

He broke the spell. "So, Thomas, would you like to step outside and take a gander at our ship? We weigh anchor at first light, headed to India and beyond."

We left the boisterous bunch in the pub and walked out into a star-filled night. With sails furled, the tall masts stood like soldiers at attention while the hull blended into the dark sea. I stood for a moment in quiet awe, wondering what it must be like to sail half-way around the world, not seeing anyone other than your crew mates for weeks on end.

Conrad broke the silence. "So, Thomas, what questions do you have for me?"

I stammered. I had been pursuing a very different train of thought. "I-I'm not sure. Maybe, how – or why – did you first get started telling stories? I mean, sure, now everyone listens to you because you're really good, but I doubt you started out like that. Where did you get the courage to start telling your stories?"

"I was driven to it, Thomas. *The artist creates because he must. He is so much of a voice that, for him, silence is like death.* I can tell from the way you listened that you have the drive too. Go back and start writing. The stories are waiting for you to give them a voice."

We wandered along the pier for a while, Conrad giving me a taste of life at sea and a few more hints about writing, until it was time for me to head back.

The tour, the tavern, the whole evening swirled around my head as I fell into my small cot later that night.

# Six

The little copper bell hanging above the door dinged the arrival of a customer. I put down my coffee and looked up. A woman and a boy were standing in the doorway, dripping rainwater on the rug, and collapsing an umbrella.

"Welcome," I said. "Come on in out of the weather. You can stick the umbrella in the stand with mine."

The woman dropped the hood of her coat and looked around. When she did, the breath was sucked out of my lungs - she was a dead ringer for Chantelle, the lady I was sent to buy butter from in Paris. She possessed the same statuesque demeanor but unlike her French counterpart, this woman had her hair pulled back, and wore oversized reading glasses.

The boy at her side was speaking and finally, caught my attention. He was asking, "Do you have any books on ice hockey?"

Pulling myself together, I focused upon the lad. "Ice hockey? Sure, come look over here." I led him to the section on sports, wherein the bottom shelf was hockey. "Anything in particular?" I asked.

"Goalie. I'm a goalie."

"No kidding. Me too."

With that opening, we dove into the nitty-gritty details of pulling on the pads and standing in front of a

6'x4' opening, trying to stop a hard rubber disk known as a puck. I thought I recalled Ken Dryden's book about his career as a goal tender for the Montreal Canadians but couldn't find it. After a brief search, the boy opted for the only book we had on the position: *The Hockey Goalie's Handbook : An Authoritative Guide for Players and Coaches* by Jim Corsi.

Together we walked back to the sales counter. The woman emerged from the stacks and took out a credit card.

"Your son and I have something in common. We are both ice hockey goalies," I said, my best attempt at a charming smile. "Quite a coincidence being that we're in North Carolina where hockey is uncommon."

"Nephew."

"Nephew?"

"He's my sister's son."

"Oh!"

Clearly my face betrayed my thoughts, a weakness of mine that made me an abysmal poker player. My eyes flicked down to her left hand, no ring on her ring finger.

She smiled.

"Well," I said, a tad flustered. "That'll be twelve ninety-nine."

As they were buttoning up against the steady rain outside, I said, "Oh by the way. Don't forget your..." I jotted a note on a store business card, "...Frequent Shoppers Discount. Here you go."

I handed the card to the woman.

Adjusting her glasses, she gave it a quick look. "Wow. Fifty percent off on my next purchase. Thank you. That must really be kicking sales into high gear!"

"Well, not yet."

"Not yet? You're kidding. How long has the special been running?"

"It just started."

She and I locked eyes. It was one of those 'you don't have to say anything' moments.

She smiled.

I smiled and shrugged.

Then she stepped outside, opened her umbrella, and they were gone.

After they left, I remembered the pile of sports books that had just come into the store a few days prior, and with a dope slap to the side of my head, hustled over the spiral stairs where they were stacked. Sure enough, there, about halfway down in the pile was Ken Dryden's book, *The Game*.

"Well," I thought. "Maybe they'll come back."

I carried the book to the sales counter and flipped through it. Then a lightbulb went on inside my head.

"I wonder."

After the office was closed, I went straight home, ate some macaroni and cheese that had been in the refrigerator for a dangerously long time, and then plopped down on my bed. The suitcases stood over against the wall, as always, silently calling to me. I held Dryden's book and went over the events of the recent past. First, I touch the suitcases. That seems to open some weird sort of portal. And when I don't physically touch them, I go nowhere. And when I do travel, I always go to a place that is alive in my subconscious. Same with time-frame, it works the same way. Now, I tightly gripped the book, said aloud, "I wonder if I can control this crazy thing."

I jumped to my feet, crossed the space to where the suitcases stood, and reached down and touched the large one. There it was again, that same tingling in my hands and slight blurring of my vision. Then it passed. I backed away, flopped back down onto my bed, fluffed up my pillow, and began reading.

Instantly, the smell of the disinfectant used on the rubber floor covering brought back memories of my ice hockey days which began with Pee Wee teams. It was always the same. There must be only one cleaning product manufacturer in the world because every locker room smelled the same. No exception.

This mat kept the sharp hockey skate blades from being dulled by walking upon concrete, and the variety of liquids (sweat, saliva, blood, and all sorts of other human secretions that would be best not listed) must be cleaned-off daily. If not, bad things happen.

Nonetheless, the first deep breath upon walking through the door transformed me back to all the years suiting up in the company of fellow teammates. Although the locker room was nearly empty, in my mind's eye just for a passing moment, the benches which wrapped around along the walls were full. There were 8-year-old kids and college undergrads and grown men, seated side by side, excitedly laughing and joking and lacing up their skates. All in all, not a bad place to be.

I sat on the bench next to a goalie. It was unmistakably Ken Dryden, le gardien de hockey for the Montreal Canadians. He was in his long underwear; his pile of equipment scattered on the floor at his feet.

He looked at me, smiled and extended his hand.

"You must be Thomas," he said.

"I am." *I wonder how lame it would be if I asked him for his autograph?*

"Thanks for comin'."

There were already a few other players in the locker room. They were drifting in, one by one. Goalies are always the first to arrive for practices or games, as they have way more equipment to pull on than the other players, and it takes longer.

As each player entered, they looked our way, spied me, nodded, and a bit curiously said, "Bonjour."

One fellow, a burly sort missing a few teeth and with a red scar on his chin, asked "Qui c'est?"

"He's the guy I was tellin' you about," Ken replied.

The burly guy nodded, his face softened, and he smiled at me. He looked all the world like some grizzly jack o lantern, but I didn't dare tell him. I smiled back.

"Où sont vos patins?"

I furrowed my brow. "My skates?"

Dryden pulled on his socks, fastening the tops to a garter clip.

"Yeah, I told the guys that you were going to play for me tonight."

"Wha..."

He grinned. "No worries. I've got this."

He then slipped his feet into his heavily padded pants, stood, and pulled the suspenders up onto his shoulders.

"Did you say something about playing for you tonight?"

Dryden sat back down and took his skates out of his duffle bag. He stared at them. "Last week," he began, his voice lower, still staring at his blades. "I sort of lost it." He turned and looked at me. His face had pain written all over. "I came unglued after our loss in the first game against the Bruins. It was my fault." He exhaled heavily. "I didn't know if I could ever suit up again. That's why I sent for you."

"Me?"

"Yeah." Dryden smiled. "We're not exactly the same size but when you're all suited up, no one would know the difference. You're a goalie. I'm a goalie. Once you pull on my mask..." He shrugged.

It took a while for my mouth, which was wordlessly moving, to create sounds. "You've got to be kidding me. You're the world's best, I'm just a hack."

Dryden laughed, as he pulled on his skates, and began tightening the laces. "You would have done fine. Hell, I gave up three bunnies in that game. You'd have stopped *them*, I'm sure of it."

I sat, open mouthed, unable to speak.

Hockey goalies are the last line of defense in this game invented by Canada, a fact that is cherished by all Canadians with fierce pride. When a goalie is on, he is the hero. But when the goalie is off his game and bunnies – easy shots that should be saved - hop by into the net, they become the quintessential goat. It doesn't matter what you did yesterday. All that matters is 'did you stop the puck or not?' This is a position that is not for the faint of heart.

I sat back and shook my head slowly. My bowels

were about to explode just imagining suiting up, walking to the rink, and skating into my goal.

Dryden laughed. Then reached down, pulled on his enormous goalie leg pads, and began buckling them up. "Been there, done that." He joined me, leaning back against the wall, and got serious again. "I really was finished you know. That's why I sent for you." He stared down at his hands, for a few silent beats, then said, "But somehow, I reached down into my gut and found..."

I waited for him to finish.

But he didn't finish. After a few more beats, he looked over at me and smiled, then grabbed his padded chest protector and slid his torso into it.

The locker room door flew open and a man dressed in a suit stepped in, yelled "DEUX MINUTES!" then ducked back out again.

Dryden took a few cleansing breaths then pulled his red Montreal Canadians sweater over his head. "Oh, by the way..." He reached into his duffle bag, took out an envelope, and handed it to me. "These are for you. My way of saying thanks."

I opened the envelope. Inside were two tickets for each of the remaining playoff games. The street value to these tickets was more than I could imagine. Thousands? Maybe more?

"Wow," I said weakly. "You didn't have to..."

"Yeah, I did."

I looked around the locker room. The world was poised for action and holding its breath, waiting for the word, ready to begin, the tension crackling. Then the door opened again, and all the players yelled. Dryden leaped to his feet, grabbed his stick and gloves and mask, reached over, and shook my hand, then led his team out onto the ice of the Montreal Forum.

The building exploded with all the noise 18,076 rabid French-Canadian fans could make. Then came the playing of the Star-Spangled Banner, followed by the Canadian National anthem, O' Canada. All 18,076 belted out every word; *"...O' Canada, we stand on guard for thee..."*. Then the horn sounded, the referee blew his whistle, and the puck was dropped.

I kept thinking about what he had said, but somehow, I reached down into my gut and found... found what? Courage? Resolve? Daring? Is this how it's done?

Shakily, I got to my feet and left the locker room. I had to go find my seat.

# SEVEN

I startled awake in the middle of the night in my own bed. Well, four in the morning, but feeling happy. No, not happy. Content. Lying in the darkness, I recalled my evening of pure fulfillment watching my hero play a stellar hockey game. I marvel at the ease of my recollection, convinced of another spectacular, otherworldly experience. How could I believe that I spent last night in Canada with the great Ken Dryden, playing a championship game in 1977? It's 2019, for Pete's sake. But it seemed so real. Sure wish I could use the rest of those playoff game tickets.

"Wait a minute. I wonder... ." Throwing off the covers and scrambling down to the end of my bed, I hesitated to touch the three bags, but I had to know, I had to look. And there they were, two playoff game tickets resting across medium's handle. "I knew it. I did go!" But these tickets were for over thirty years ago. What purpose would they serve now?

I needed to think about this. Did Ken mean for me to go to these games somehow? If I believe—no, I know--I attended a 1977 playoff game last night, before I was born, then why shouldn't I believe I have these tickets in my hand right now? Maybe I do have control over where I go, what I can do.

The full-length mirror in my bathroom definitely

told no lies, and I stared disgusted at my unfit physique. Stretching out my arms like Leonardo's Vitruvian Man, I knew I did not see the physically fit specimen he had envisioned. "At this point, I have to believe that anything's possible." I relieved myself, flushed the toilet and returned to my cramped bedroom, setting the clock for six a.m., determined to walk in the park for at least forty-five minutes before I headed for the bookstore.

I was tempted to roll over and ignore the annoying alarm, but I could hear Leonardo prodding me to get up. *Inaction saps the vigor of the mind.* That's what he said. And I really needed to get off my ass and think about these last few days, where I'd been and why. I fished a pair of tennis shoes out of the bottom of my closet, threw on some shorts and a t-shirt, and actually ran down the three flights of stairs.

Fifty minutes later I panted up slowly, soaking wet from perspiration. If I pushed myself, I could shower, dress and grab a decent breakfast at Lulu's Café before opening the bookstore. My walk made me wonder about the last shipment of books that came in and if there would be anything interesting for me...or for that lady with the nephew. She might come back. "Exercise sharpens the mind and invigorates the soul, Leo!"

Just before I headed out, I grabbed the playoff tickets and stuck them in my wallet.

"Good morning, Thomas. Surprised to see you so early, sitting down to eat instead of grabbing a cup of coffee to go. Turning over a new leaf?"

"Something like that, Lulu. I'll have a number two over light with coffee. How are you this morning?"

"Other than the arthritis and the bunions, I'm fine.

You look mighty spiffy this morning. That blue shirt brings out your beautiful eyes. Did you get a haircut?"

"No, no haircut, just showered and shaved."

"That's it. You shaved! You should never cover up that handsome face again. Be right back with your coffee."

After breakfast, I walked two doors down to the bookstore and opened the boxes with deliberation, hoping I could keep up my new routine. "Meow, I am going to get a haircut this afternoon. There should only be one hairy vagrant languishing pointlessly in here."

"Meow." The resident cat yawned, stretched and closed his disinterested eyes.

Three days later just before closing time, the bell over the door rang in the blonde lady. I looked up from my book and we locked eyes. I couldn't help myself. I smiled.

"Oh, thank goodness you're still open. I'm desperate for that new Louise Penny book and hoped you might have it. Do you?"

"You mean this one?" I held up the book in my hands.

"Yes, yes! You like her too? I just love the constancy of the main characters and the way she weaves her stories around the same setting. Do you have more than one copy?"

"Buy this one. You can use your Frequent Shopper Discount card. That is, if you still have it."

She opened her purse and placed the card on the counter. I punched the card and handed it back. "It's only official if you print your name on the back," I said, handing her a pen.

I rang up the sale, put the book in a bag and returned

her card. "Come back nine more times and you'll get a free book of your choice, Sherry."

"Wow. That's great. It's Cherie, though. My mother was a French teacher."

"Cherie, it is." I cocked my head, staring again into her eyes, framed by those big round glasses. "You know, you really look—"

"—familiar!" She completed my thought. "I thought so when I came in the other day with my nephew. Did you go to the university here?"

"Yeah, long time ago. You?"

"Yes, I graduated in 2008. History major. I think we might have had a class together my junior year."

Oh great, I thought. Now I have to reveal the fact that I quit, dropped out. It's time to close up shop. "Well, Cherie, we close at five on Wednesdays, and it's five, so... ."

"Good. We can grab a bite down the street. Do you ever eat at Lulu's? I just love their pastries."

"Uh, well, I don't usually—"

"Oh, c'mon. My treat. I don't even know your name."

We had coffee and pastries at Lulu's, but that wasn't enough. Cherie talked with joy and intensity and, dare I say, a song in her voice? We discovered that our paths had crossed in Dr. Lashinsky's Philosophy 281 class, required for all undeclared majors. We laughed at the suggestion that if you didn't know what you wanted to do with your life, deep thought might help. When I recalled the professor's routine at the beginning of every class, Cherie howled in a most un-ladylike fashion, and I fell in love.

"Oh, yesyesyes. That timeline! She would come in the room, pick up a piece of chalk, and draw a line all the way across the board."

I chimed in, "And then she would write BC on one end and AD on the other, and mark off time periods, and... "

We said together, "...write the names of the philosophers she had already told us about and start in with another one."

"Why don't you two get dinner somewhere?" Lulu interrupted. "We close at seven."

Had I been sitting here talking to this woman for two hours? My palms got sweaty and I just panicked. If we ended things now, I'd never see her again. She is just too smart, too quick and too good-looking to give me a second thought. "Let's get dinner. Are you hungry? Do you have plans, I mean? My treat. I know a great little Greek restaurant not too far from here. You can follow me or I can drive or ..."

"Sure Thomas. I'll follow you."

The rest of the night had to have been a dream. By the end of our meal, with a second dose of coffee and pastry for the day, Cherie had captured a spark I thought had been extinguished. Somehow, she gently pried a lot of personal stuff I had not talked about to anyone. I shamefully explained my dropout status after my father died; I really had no excuse for never going back to finish my degree. Cherie just put her hand on mine, wiped a tear from her own eye, and said, "I'm so sorry. You had a lot of grief to deal with, all by yourself." Then she applauded me for being responsible, becoming independent, and not getting buried in student debt.

That was a far cry from the reaction I got from my college crush. I had fallen head over heels for Stacy my freshman year and we were inseparable, until the moment I told her of my father's suicide, his bankrupt status, and my need to quit school and get a job. Stacy's last comment as she left my apartment, "It is very inconsiderate of you not to care that I have to go back to living in a dorm, Thomas MacDonald."

"She sounds like such a terrible person, Thomas. What did you even see in her?"

"Yeah. That's a good question. Weird as it sounds, I don't have a good answer. My Dad had come up to the campus to buy me a car, 'a flashy one, girls like that,' he had said. We were sitting in the coffee shop, Stacy overheard the conversation and chimed in something about 'understated flash, a car that speaks old money.' She giggled and mentioned we were in the same biology class. Then she walked off telling me to let her know when I got my car. My father was so taken by her, thought she would be a 'great catch' and kept after me to ask her out. So I finally did. I know it sounds stupid, but dating her seemed to make my father happy. Dad paid for an apartment my sophomore year, Stacy moved in, and the rest, as they say, is history."

"Hmm. Sounds pretty shallow. Sorry, but really."

"Oh, I don't disagree. In the moment, the sex was good and for the first time I could remember my father seemed proud of me. Then he went broke, committed suicide, and she dumped me. What a waste."

Cherie offered a glorious smile. "Well, if it makes you feel any better, I dated a jerk too. As a matter of fact, I almost married the guy. He actually came from old money and we met at a fund-raising function at the museum I worked in up in Boston. Phillipe Hancock. The THIRD." When she laughed that full laugh again, I did feel better. "Anyway, after spending a long weekend with his family, I quickly discovered what snobs they all were. Luckily, the job in Charlotte came up and I couldn't escape fast enough. And I'm glad I'm here."

I knew we couldn't stretch the evening out any longer when the lights flicked on and off. If this day was real, not a suitcase trip, I didn't want it to end.

"Gotta go, Thomas. I have a paper to finish for my on-line grad class that's due before midnight." We exchanged numbers, she pecked me on the cheek, and we drove off in different directions. I held my breath as I climbed the steps to my apartment.

Small-medium-large sat tauntingly at the end of my bed. "Not touching you tonight. I'm quite satisfied," I told my old companions. But in the middle of the night, when I got up to go the bathroom, I tripped over the biggest bag. "No!" I yelled, but the tingling had begun.

I knew I'd screwed up before I opened my eyes. The cot my body lay on, the cool natural air, the aroma of roasted chicken, feta, basil and olive oil. Coffee. Cinnamon. Was I in Rome? Cautiously, I peered through half-closed eyes and saw columns everywhere. And men in robes draped loosely across their bodies, most of them balding, white-haired, some carrying canes. One of the men approached me and I sat up, dejected that I was somewhere far, far away from Cherie.

"Good morning, Thomas. I sensed you needed to sleep before our lesson today. Do not fret, my son. You will go back home even more refreshed. You are here just for the day because it is time for you to bolster your confidence. *Know thyself*, Thomas. You are distressed because you think you don't deserve to be happy. Trust your instincts and don't worry about what others think of you."

I knew the drill by now, but I did not know who this guy was, or where I was supposed to be, or why I was here. I had wanted to listen and learn, but I had to ask, "Who are you, sir, and why am I here?"

"More importantly, who are you? Do you know? *To find yourself, think* for *yourself.* You need to take time to reflect on your worth. You are a good person, Thomas, yet you judge yourself as a failure. What is more admirable than a self-sufficient man who is kind to others, seeks knowledge, and longs for true love?"

"Yeah, well, thanks, but I don't think constantly looking for answers makes for a successful person. I'm what most people consider a loser—no career, no family, no social life, nothing I can call my own."

"Really, Thomas? You have money saved in the bank, you depend on no one for your survival, you have a roof over your head, you are eating well, finally, you are beginning to treat your body with respect—"

"Well, sorry to interrupt and I appreciate the pep talk, but I don't consider a few walks in the park and one French meal constitutes a successful person."

"Please, Thomas. You have begun. That is what is important. You have finally crawled out from under the disappointment of one lost love. *The hottest love has the coldest end.* Your father ended his life and you lost your direction. Remember that your father had one love in his life, your mother, and he sacrificed his career to support hers. That is to be admired. He just could not deal with the fact that no amount of money could keep her alive and he lost himself. You are not your father. *Know thyself*, Thomas."

I jumped up off of my cot. "You are Socrates. Socrates!" I held my head in my hands, to keep from losing my mind. I laughed at the thought of those philosophy class timelines and wondered what Cherie would say if she knew I were here.

Socrates indicated for me to walk with him, so I followed him into a garden shrouded with vines and sculptures. "I am pleased that you think of your new love, Thomas. *A good woman has much value. Once made equal to man, woman becomes his superior*, and a loved woman can enrich and fulfill a man. You have recently felt content, and nearly felt afraid, afraid that it would not last. A good man deserves to feel contentment. *Contentment is a natural wealth; luxury is artificial poverty.*

We walked among the flowers and in between columns of granite. I gave myself up to his wisdom, trying to absorb everything he said to me. For some reason he knew me and understood my misgivings, my failures. I had to take advantage of this remarkable stroll along the paths of the ancient Greeks.

Convinced that I had to continue my recent immersion into these surreal opportunities, I listened and held tight to Socrates' warning that *an unexamined life is not worth living.*

Overwhelmed with his encouragement, I almost wanted to stay, to start afresh in Athens and just grow from there, but I knew that wasn't possible. I had to return to my present life and keep moving forward. At the end of the day, the old gentleman put his hand on my shoulder and looked directly into my eyes. "Thomas, *falling down is not a failure. Failure comes when you stay where you have fallen.*"

# EIGHT

A fter last night, I decided to pursue my new regimen with increased vigor. As I ran along the Greenway, I felt myself coming alive – the crisp fall air, the leaves just beginning to turn, the birds calling back and forth. Why had I not noticed all of this before?

I was whistling as I opened the door to the shop. Yes, whistling. I don't remember doing that since I first mastered the art back in third grade. No new books to sort, and not likely to be disturbed by customers unless Cherie stopped by to get another punch in her card. After completing my morning routine fixing up the shop, I decided to try to revive my new-found interest in writing. My new librarian friend would surely be impressed by literary talent, assuming, of course, that I could put to use some of the advice I had gleaned from Charles and Joseph.

Conrad had said, *"The artist creates because he must."* Well, I certainly didn't consider myself an artist, but I felt a growing need to get words down on paper. I kept trying to write a story with Cherie as my heroine, but I came up short. I didn't know her well enough. I didn't know what she would say or do. I didn't know much about her background. But I did know one person very well – me. I found myself writing about a young boy who was afraid to try new things, a boy who could never live up to his father's expectations, a boy who watched his mother – the only one who seemed to have faith in him – die slowly and painfully. And I stopped worrying whether it was "polished," or it would impress anybody. I was writing for myself, and as I wrote, I started to understand a little bit more about this person at the other end of the pen.

A couple of customers actually did come in; they didn't buy anything, of course, but it passed some time. I pulled myself away from my writing and decided to try to make the bookstore more exciting and interesting by rearranging the displays. That way customers could find what they wanted without having to paw through random stacks of books.

All day, I found myself looking out the window, up and down the street, willing Cherie to burst through the door bringing the sunshine in with her. I figured I'd wait until she got home from work and give her a call. Maybe she'd be up for dinner tonight – or tomorrow – or the weekend.

I reached into my wallet to retrieve the card on which she had carefully written her number. NO! That couldn't be! I emptied the contents of my wallet and pored through everything twice – and once again. I checked my pockets. Maybe it had fallen out somewhere in my apartment.

As soon as I got home, heart pounding, I checked everything – under the cushions, in the garbage, in my closet. It was gone. I plunked down on the couch, the old Thomas stealing in and sitting beside me, whispering "Loser, jerk, fool. What made you think she would be interested in the likes of you?"

I looked over at the suitcases and thought about just taking a trip and maybe not coming back. But with my luck, I'd probably end up in the middle of a gang war or something.

The next day went by similarly, trying unsuccessfully to write, watching for Cherie, coming home and wallowing in my despair. But then I saw all my mentors – Leonardo, Charles, Julia, Joseph, Ken, and Socrates – shaking their heads in disappointment and saying, "We taught you better than this. Stop feeling sorry for yourself. *Face it.*"

The following morning, I got up early, took an extra-long run, channeling positive energy the whole way. When I got to the shop, I found a new shipment of books that needed to be sorted and enticingly displayed. The morning passed quickly.

Shortly after noon, the bell rang. When I looked up, my mouth went dry. There was Cherie, looking more beautiful than ever.

"Thomas," she called a little tentatively.

"Cherie," I stammered,What are you doing here? I mean, I didn't expect to see you now. I mean . . . oh shit! Hi Great to see you."

Her laugh was pure music and her smile lit up the whole bookstore.

"When you didn't call, I was afraid that maybe you didn't have as good a time as I did the other night."

"Oh God no," I stammered. "It's just that I . . ."

"But I decided to take a chance and see for myself what's going on."

"Oh my gosh, I am so glad to see you." I wanted to give her a huge hug, but I settled for grasping her hand and staring into her beautiful eyes. "I lost your number. I don't know what happened. I looked every-where – in my pockets, under the cushions – Oh God, I'm babbling." I stopped, took a deep breath, and never taking my eyes off her, I said, "It's great to see you."

She smiled that amazing smile. "Good to see you too. Actually, I came in to see if you had any books on The Smokies. An old friend of mine and I are going there this weekend to do some hiking. The weather is supposed to be perfect and the leaves are . . . "

I didn't hear any more. All I heard was "old friend." Right. Probably some guy who has been trying to get together with her for years.

"This friend of yours," I stammered, "is he a big hiker too?"

Cherie laughed. "Oh dear, dear Thomas. Just like a man. You assume that we women can't take care of ourselves in the big bad wilderness. As it happens, he's a she, and yes, she's a great hiker. We worked to-gether one summer for the AMC, helping to repair the Appalachian trail in the White Mountains.

"But when I get back, we'll definitely get together."

Hiking, hmm. That was going to be a tough one. My sole experience with crawling around in the great out-doors was our fifth-grade trip to Crowders Mountain. All I remember about it is sliding down a rocky slope, badly scraping my knee and elbow and one side of my face, and crying, while Butch Delgado, my arch enemy, and his crew laughed at me.

But hey, if there's one thing I've learned from all my trips, it's that I can do all kinds of things that I never be-lieved possible. First I needed to find out what the hell the AMC was where Cherie worked that summer. My google search revealed that it was not likely the movie chain, but rather the Appalachian Mountain Club, a big hiking organization. Then I checked out "hiking the Appalachian Trail." Wow! It's 2,190 miles long and some people hike the whole thing in one year! Good grief! These were the people Cherie was meeting when she worked with the AMC. Pretty impressive. I was a long, long way from anything like that, but I could certainly start with some baby steps.

I sat down and made a plan. If I could get into shape, maybe eventually Cherie and I could do a little exploration – get out by ourselves, far away from everybody.

- Climb up and down the three flights of stairs to apartment several times every day, starting with three
- Extend my morning jog along the Greenway
- Read up on nearby hikes
- Join a gym

I looked at my list and harrumphed. Given my past history, not likely to happen, but this is the new me, and I'll do what I can.

On my third trip up the stairs, Crystal emerged from her office, and said, "Thomas, what the hell are you doing?"

"Just getting in shape, Crystal. You ought to give it a try."

I think I heard her murmur something like, "What a jerk!. Glad I got rid of him."

Later that night, I decided I was ready to see where the suitcases would take me. I still hadn't quite figured out just exactly how they decided my next adventure, but I was definitely ready. I entered the bedroom, took a deep breath, gave medium a gentle tap, and felt a slight tingling. Then I lay down and fell asleep.

I woke up to a cool breeze fanning my cheek and rustling leaves overhead. When I opened my eyes, I gasped at the beauty of the forest surrounding me. Where was I?

"It's about time you woke up, young man," the slightly raspy voice of an old woman said. "I need to get moving. I have to get to the hut before it gets dark."

I sat up and looked into the face of a small dynamo of a woman. She was a bit on the dumpy side, not the super-fit type you would expect to find hiking out here alone. Wisps of gray hair stuck out from the kerchief she had wrapped around her head, and her eyes smiled from a nest of wrinkles. She wore a pair of brown pants and a buttoned-up shirt and had a sack like a duffle bag slung over her shoulder and a walking stick in her hand. And on her feet, not sturdy hiking boots, but a pair of flimsy sneakers.

She read the confusion on my face and laughed. "C'mon. Get up and let's get going. We can talk on the way."

She spoke with such authority that I jumped up and fell in behind her as she started up the trail.

"Thomas, I've never been one to beat around the bush. I'm Emma Gatewood, generally referred to as Grandma Gatewood. I've been on this bloomin' trail for about 4 months now. Started in Georgia. I must say, the *National Geographic* article I read made it sound a lot easier than it's been. *I would never have started this trip if I had known how tough it was, but I couldn't and wouldn't quit.* And my oh my, what I would have missed if I had."

Oh my gosh. I was hiking with the woman who was said to have saved the Appalachian Trail. Every site I googled on "hiking the Appalachian Trail," or "people who hiked the AT" had told the story of Grandma Gatewood, a 67-year-old woman who set out in 1955 on the 2,000+ mile hike with just an army blanket, a raincoat, a change of clothes, and a shower curtain in her sack, and soon became a celebrity. She used her new-found celebrity status to goad governments into improving the trail, which had become woefully neglected, and people began to think, "If this old lady can hike the trail, I can too." Being a thru-hiker – hiking from Georgia to Maine in a single year - became the goal of many, who soon found it to be a daunting task, and they had new admiration for Grandma Gatewood.

I was already starting to get winded trying to keep up with her. The trail had suddenly gotten a lot steeper, and I found myself grabbing on to saplings along the path to pull myself up.

She turned around and smiled. "You can do this, Thomas. Just keep pushing through. Not too much farther till we reach the top, and then there will be a beautiful view."

When I looked up, I saw a rock ledge rising in front of me. I stood, catching my breath and shaking my head. No way could I get up that!

"It's not as bad as it looks. The trail usually skirts the worst of it and there will be steps. Have faith, Thomas."

Faith?! I needed magic. Maybe if I had started my fitness plan several weeks ago, or maybe if the damn

ALAN MULAK, DONNA SMITH, SUE PASCUCCI

suitcases had landed me on the top of the mountain instead of here, I could make it.

Grandma stood a few feet above me, smiling and nodding, holding her hand out to me.

I took a few deep breaths and followed her.

About a half hour later, we reached the top, and I flopped down on the rocky crest, almost too exhausted to appreciate the view. Almost. Even in my semi-comatose state, though, I was blown away by what opened up before me. I had seen pictures and movies of mountain-top vistas, of course, but I had no idea how far they were from the magnificence of reality.

My mouth dropped open. "It's amazing!" I managed to squeak out with the little bit of breath I had left.

"This is what keeps me going," Grandma said softly, respecting the sanctity of the moment. "Each view is unique. It's like a being a little closer to heaven."

We sat quietly for a moment, then she took out her canteen and handed it to me. I wanted to drain the whole thing; I hadn't realized how thirsty I was, but I just took a few gulps, thankful for her generosity.

I looked over at her as she sat looking out at the mountains stretched out before us. I had so many questions that I didn't know where to begin.

I started with, "Where are we?"

"We're on the top of Mount Madison in the White Mountains of New Hampshire. Getting near the end of the trail, though I understand there are some heart-breakers ahead. When I started out on this hike," she said, looking off into the distance, "I told my kids I was just going for a walk. They would have tried to stop me - all eleven of them – if they knew what I was doing. They would have thought I was crazy. And people I've met along the way always ask me, 'Why are you doing this?' They figure there must be some hidden reason. But I say, 'Because it was there,' or 'It seemed like a lark,' or something like that."

"Is that the real reason?" I asked, now captivated by this feisty woman.

"Yes – and no. People are much more complicated than that. I was looking for healing for some deeply buried wounds from long ago – from an abusive husband. I figured if I could survive broken ribs, knocked-out teeth, bloodied noses, and forced labor, I could tackle this, and maybe find a way to become whole again."

"Did it work?" My question sounded both naïve and intrusive.

She took a moment, then said, "I discovered that *if you go to the mountains, and sleep on the leaf carpeted floors And enjoy the bigness of nature And the beauty of all out-of-doors, You'll find your troubles all fading.*"

She looked at me to make sure that I had heard her message. Then she laughed. "But I must say that it wasn't all nature and beauty. I came across a few mountain lions and bears that gave me a pretty good scare. And a rattlesnake almost had its way with me. And a couple of hurricanes. But I kept pushing on."

"Weren't you afraid? I mean, bears and mountain lions and even some pretty creepy humans you must have met along the way."

"*If I'd been afraid I never would have started out in the first place.*"

I looked at Grandma with admiration. I wanted desperately to hear more of her story, but I was exhausted. She continued talking, but I could no longer hear anything. My eyes closed, and the rock beneath me felt as soft and comfortable as my old king-sized bed back home.

And indeed, when I next opened my eyes, that's precisely where I was. As I started to get up, I groaned. Who knew you had so many leg muscles – and all of them could be in agony at the same time? I guess it takes more than a few runs up and down the stairs to make an experienced hiker. I thought about Grandma Gatewood and how many mountains she had climbed – at age 67, no less – and how many days she had been pushing on, carrying her funny sack over her shoulder. She must have wanted to just crawl back under her blanket and sleep the day away sometimes. But she kept on. I could too.

When I got to the bookstore, I found a book on *Easy Hikes in North_Carolina._*I checked out those in the greater Charlotte area and found a couple that sounded like I could handle – once I was able to actually move my legs. Maybe next weekend I could convince Cherie to take one of them with me. I wasn't going to impress her with my hiking prowess, but what a great atmosphere to get to really know each other.

Tuesday a little after noon, the bell rang and Cherie stepped in, bringing the sunshine with her. She chattered about how wonderful her hiking weekend had been and how much she had missed actually getting out in nature and pushing herself to go a little further than she thought she could go. I laughed when she said, "And I found I few muscles I had forgotten about," and rubbed my still-recovering quads.

"Um, Cherie. I just came across this book." I held up
*Easy Hikes in North Carolina.* "I know you're a much
more experienced hiker than I am, but I wondered if
you might be interested in trying one of these with me
this Sunday." There. I did it. I asked her.

"I'd love it!" She replied. "Something a little less
challenging would be welcome after this past weekend.
Anne Marie and I have always had a competitive relationship, so we really pushed each other. Some time to
really enjoy nature – and each other," she blushed a
little when she said this, "would be delightful."

On the one hand, the week flew by. I needed more
time to get my aching legs into better shape so I wouldn't
embarrass myself. On the other hand, it seemed to take
forever. I couldn't wait to be out in the woods with the
one person I wanted to share my life with.

"C'mon, slow poke," Cherie laughed. "We're almost
to the top, and you're going to love the view." I was
right. A week wasn't enough time for me to be able to
keep up with this experienced hiker. However, at least I
wasn't disgracing myself. And we had been able to chat
along the way – just ordinary chit-chat, about weather
and work and life in Charlotte, the kind of comfortable
conversation that good friends have.

In my dreams, I would have shouted, "Race you to
the top!" and zipped past her. Instead I said, "Just taking some time to enjoy *the bigness of nature and the
beauty of all outdoors.*"

"Good answer – and good excuse for lagging behind," she laughed again, and gave my hand a squeeze
when I caught up to her.

This time, when I made it to the top of the mountain, I had the energy to stand and take in the view.

"Amazing, isn't it," Cherie said. "It's one reason I love hiking – a reward for pushing through. Wouldn't it be nice if all of life was like that? You struggle and persist, and then you get to sit back and soak up the beauty?"

"I'm beginning to think that at least sometimes it's like that." I looked over at her, but she was lost in thought – her mind somewhere down in the valley.

"Sometimes. Fortunately. But not always."

I waited. I didn't want to pry into the dark corners of her life, but if she would let me in, I was willing to go.

"Most of the young people who worked at the AMC were there because they loved hiking and the outdoors, but a surprising number were, like me, running away from something, hoping to find healing in the mountains."

She was still looking wistfully at the panorama before us. "Did it work?" I asked hesitantly.

"For the most part. After that summer - and a good bit of therapy - I have been able to put some pretty nasty stuff behind me."

She wasn't going to give me any more details. Not yet, anyway. She looked so "together," so normal. I wondered if anybody had that "Brady-Bunch" life. Maybe we're all a little screwed up. Maybe I wasn't alone.

I said, "I guess Grandma Gatewood was right when she said, 'If you can *enjoy the bigness of nature and the beauty of all out-of-doors, you'll find your troubles all fading.*'" I got momentarily lost in my memories of that feisty little old woman who had shown me so much, and the wonders of that whole trip.

Then I looked over at Cherie. She was staring at me, open-mouthed. "How do you know about Grandma Gatewood? She's not exactly a household name."

Shit! I hadn't meant to let that out. I blushed and stammered, "Um, I just read about her, you know. Like, when I looked up stuff on hiking." I wasn't prepared for this. "You know, she just comes up when you google the Appalachian Trail – I mean, people who hike the trail."

"Thomas, what's going on? Why did you get so flustered when I just asked you a simple question? This isn't the first time it's happened. Is there something you aren't telling me?"

"No, no, no, Cherie. I don't know. I just do stupid things sometimes. Please don't be upset." I looked so helpless, I guess she took pity on me.

She smiled and said, "Okay. Let's start back. I'm getting a bit chilled."

# NINE

With more than a bit of a spring in my step, I took the stairs to the third floor of the Charlotte Mecklenburg Public Library at 4:00 pm sharp. Cherie had called and invited me out to dinner when she got off work at about 5:00. But first, she wanted to show me around her workplace.

A date! A real date! A shower and shave and wear a clean shirt date!

But when I met her at the entrance to the Ancestry Research and Reference Department, she was wringing her hands.

"I'm sorry but we've been asked to sit in on an interview with a candidate for the new director. I'll be an hour or so."

My shoulders sagged. "It's okay. I'll kill some time looking around until you're done," I said with false cheerfulness.

Cherie smiled weakly. "Thanks for being understanding. Why don't you take a workstation and research your family lineage?"

"Ya, sure," I replied. She's into this. Take an interest. She'll be impressed.

I settled in, and using Cherie's log on, rolled up my sleeves. The screen prompts were blinking.

"I won't be long...I hope." Then she turned and disappeared into a conference room.

*Name.*

No problem.

*Parents' names. Mother's maiden name. Grandparents' names.*

That was about it. It dawned on me; I really don't know much about my family. And now, with both my parents long gone, I had no one to ask. "Well," I mumbled. "Here goes."

I hit enter.

After a moment, the screen came back with this message:

*Preliminary search results: The number of records exceeds the maximum of one million. Refine search. Suggest entering known relative from past.*

I sat back. More than one million MacDonald records? Wow. A known relative? Hmm. Wait a minute, didn't dad used to talk about his great uncle Duncan who was a Lieutenant Colonel or something in WWI? He had his medals. This guy would be a blood-line relative. He was in...in...Scotland's Coldstream Guards! Yeah, that was it.

I typed: Lieutenant Colonel Duncan MacDonald, Scotland Coldstream Guards. WWI.

Another moment passed.

*Search Result: significant biography available. Hit enter to print. Hit Control C to continue back in time.*

"Okay," I said quietly. "Let's keep going back."

Control C.

*Preliminary search results: The number of records exceeds the maximum of one million. Refine search. Suggest entering known relative from past.*

"You've got to be kidding me. Okay then, let's try this."

I typed: MacDonald from 1800 to 1899.

*Preliminary search results: The number of records exceeds the maximum of one million. Refine search. Suggest entering known relative from past.*

"Hmm."

I typed: MacDonald from 1700 to 1799.

*Preliminary search results: The number of records exceeds two hundred thousand. Refine search. Suggest entering known relative from past.*

I frowned. All right then, let's try: (1) MacDonald from 1700 to 1799 (2) Scotland only.

*Preliminary search results: The number of records exceeds one hundred thousand. Refine search. Suggest entering known relative from past.*

I drummed my fingers on the table and mumbled, "Never knew my family was that popular. Let's see. What about famous? Nope. There's likely no such category. How about infamous? Same thing. Legendary? Criminal? Scientist? Nope, nope, nope. How about politicians? Hmm, that might work. What would that have been called in the 1700's? King? Queen? Or how about simply Royalty?"

I typed: MacDonald from 1700 to 1799 (2) Scotland only (3) Royalty.

*Preliminary search results: The number of records is fifty-seven*

"Well. How about that! Now we're getting somewhere."

(1) MacDonald from 1700 to 1799 (2) Scotland only (3) Royalty (4) female

*Preliminary search results: The number of records is four*

*Note: Bloodline termination in three of four. Refer to Book 962-31 in stacks.*

I leaned back in my chair, muttering, "What the hell? What stacks?"

Then I looked around the room I was sitting in: I was surrounded by row after row of reference books, in shelves floor to ceiling. The sign at the end of each row read STACKS – LIBRARY STAFF ONLY.

About five minutes later, I pulled down a dusty, massive volume labelled 962-31 and plopped it down upon a nearby table. It took another few minutes to find the MacDonald "bloodline termination," and I began reading. The first three ladies were MacDonald women all right but became royalty due to their marital unions with some big deal in the royal court. They married well! But the last one, a Caillen Fergusson-MacDonald was a queen. A queen! No shit!

Her bio was the stuff rags to riches stories were made of. It made for a captivating read. This woman was from non-royal lineage and though her years as queen were somewhat obscure, she brought health and vibrancy to Scotland via canals, RR's, health measures (via washing streets and public places), and protection of drinking water, which kept cholera and the plague out of Scottish cities, etc.

I sent the bio of Queen Caillen to the printer. It was twelve pages!

In a twinkling, an hour had passed. When Cherie came out of the conference room, I never even heard her approach.

She looked stricken. "We're going to be calling the potential director's references. It's going to take a long time. I'm so very, very sorry but I must postpone our dinner. How about a raincheck?"

I didn't want to tell her how enjoyable the past hour

had been for me and how excited I was feeling about my discovery, so I gave her my best 'I understand' face and just said, "Hey, no problem. Call me when you have time."

"Promise."

I went straight home, handled the suitcases, then stretched out on my bed with something of great interest to read: the bio of my ancestor, Caillen the Queen of Scotland.

The next morning, I awoke to the sound of ducks and chickens, and the fetid odor of mammal urine filling the room.

I lay in the half-light of dawn, listening, and wrinkling my nose to the smell. The window by my bed was a rough rectangular opening in the stone wall. I swung my feet to the floor and went to stand but sat back down. My back was howling. I tried to stretch and twist slowly and it helped a bit, but this ache was going to need some time. I felt the mattress; it was clumpy and hard. That, plus all the aches and pains from my recent hiking, no wonder my back was unhappy! Again, I made to stand, this time with caution. So far, so good.

Poking my head out the window, I had hoped the fresh air would smell better. Much to my dismay, it was worse. The cobblestone street below was strewn with drippings and droppings from who knows what. Directly under my window was an enormous, fly covered Ox. I pulled my shirt over my nose, muttering, "I think I found the source of at least some of this wretched odor."

I looked to my left in time to see the occupant of the next room over emptying a bed pan down to the street, where it splattered with a yellow splosh.

Then came a loud banging on my door.

Retreating from the window, I swung open the barn-board door. There stood a young girl, perhaps eight or nine, with a riot of carrot red hair. Her dress was soiled and there was mud on her cheek, but she wore a devil-may-care smile that made me ignore her unkempt appearance.

"My mum is waitin'. Come on." Then she turned and flew down the stone stairs.

I blinked a few times, shrugged, then followed. All I could think was "here we go again."

As I stepped outside, the sun had broken through the morning fog. The ox which I had spied a moment ago, was hitched to a hay wagon, on which lay an exceedingly pregnant woman with piercing green eyes and some fashion of head wreath made from a green leafy plant – perhaps sage.

"Thomas?"

"Yes," I replied.

"Jump up," she said, patting the hay by her side.

I climbed aboard, and plopped down and as I did, the little girl with the carrot curls joined the driver, a frumpy elderly woman who held the reins in her boney hands.

"Let's off," the soon-to-be-mother said over her shoulder.

With the shake of the leather reins, the ox plodded

forward, scattering ducks and geese and chickens, all protesting loudly, as we went.

Again, I covered my face with my shirt, trying in vain to wade off the noisome stench.

"Lovely, isn't it?" the pregnant woman said, removing her sage wreath and placing it over her face.

"No, not at all."

Mercifully, we soon passed through a dark alley, and when we emerged back into the sunshine, it was a different world. The street was freshly washed and shone in the bright sun. The smell diminished as the creaking wagon rolled forward.

"Welcome to Healthy Cap and Feather Close, home to my family," she said, putting the sage back on her head. "And where are my manners. I'm Lady Provost Barbara Fergusson and my daughter is Dallen," she pointed over her shoulder at the little girl who turned and smiled, "And that's Molly, my midwife. I'm keeping her close by these days." She rubbed her belly.

The old woman held up a liver-spotted hand. "Ola."

"Ola?"

"It means hello," said Barbara.

"Okay," I said. "Ola." Then after a moment, I asked, "Where did you say we are?"

"Healthy Cap and Feather Close," Lady Provost said. "It's a section of Edinburg's Royal Mile. Think of it as a village. And that dark alley we went through, we call those vennels. And by the way, call me Barbara. I'm the first woman Provost here."

"Provost?"

"Similar to your mayor."

"I get it," but thought, *my mayor?*

"What did you think of the Royal Mile? That's where you slept last night."

I frowned. "Well, let's put it this way. This place, Healthy Cap and whatever, is much more agreeable. And smells better, too."

She smiled. Her green eyes shone. "Thank you. That's quite a compliment."

We had passed from shops on both sides of the stone road, and now were moving into a more rural setting. A large field was on the right upon which children were playing. They were tossing some sort of animal hide covered ball. It occurred to me that I was likely viewing a predecessor to rugby or soccer.

"I have to ask what may seem to be a strange question but are you Queen Caillen Fergusson-MacDonald?"

She laughed heartily. "No, not hardly." Then she covered her belly with both hands. "My babe here, kicks when I laugh."

Turning to the front of the wagon, she said, "Dallen. Hop down and go play with the kids."

Without a pause, Dallen jumped to the ground and ran out with the others.

Turning back to me, she said, "As for the queen, you will meet her in a wee while. But first, I need to show you something."

We rolled along until we came to a crossroad. A well-worn dirt trail crossed the stone road. Perched on the left was a flat stone, erected as some sort of monument.

"Hold up Molly."

We did.

"Thomas, if you would, climb down and read the words on that clach."

"Clach?"

"Flat stone. Here in Scotland we have this habit of standing flat stones all over the countryside."

With more than a little stiffness from the lumpy bed I'd slept in the previous night, I performed a controlled fall from the wagon, regained my dignity, then stepped over to the clach.

I read aloud,

*Now stairhead critics, senseless fools,*
*Censure their aim, and pride their rules*

*From Auld Reekie by Robert Fergusson*

I turned and looked at Barbara. The puzzled look upon my face must have answered her question.

"I can see you are unfamiliar with *Auld Reekie*. And what about Robert Fergusson?"

"Nope."

"How about Robert Burns?"

"Him I've heard of. A poet if I recall."

"Burns tells everyone that it was Fergusson who influenced him to become the poet he is today. Robert Fergusson was my brother." She paused. A breeze played upon her hair. "He died at the age of twenty-four. Alone. In an asylum."

"Wow. I'm sorry."

"No worries. We hadn't a word for years prior. He went one way and joined up with his companions, depression and despondency, and I went the other." She sighed. "He lived a reckless, bohemian life, getting booted out of several schools and failing at every undertaking. He took to drink and whoring and kept company with the worst lads, hanging around in the dregs of the Royal Mile. But before his fall, for a fleeting moment, he was a brilliant poet, and his masterpiece was *Auld Reekie*. That's a few lines on the clach."

I shook my head slowly.

The breeze freshened.

"Now, climb back up here and let's go meet the Queen."

We turned around and headed back to the field where the children were playing. While we rolled along, Barbara told me her tale.

"All Healthy Cap and Feather Close was as filthy and fetid as Royal Mile. I lost two children to sickness that I'm sure they caught from the piss and droppings on our roads. Every year we had plagues come whipping through our homes. It was no way to live."

With great effort, she moved her expanded belly in my direction to face me as she spoke. She brushed a handful of red hair from her face.

"I knew in my bones that we were better than hogs, so I got myself elected Lady Provost and my first task was to make it right. We dammed up a wee branch of River Tay up in the hills near Arthur's Seat, and use its waters to flush the cobbled stone streets, washing the refuse down into the lower pastures. Never have they been so lush, and the hogs and cattle grow fat there. And now our streets are clean, and our children don't get sick anymore when they play outside. And a woman with child," she patted her stomach, "can expect to have healthy young'uns."

We were approaching the field and halted. For a minute or so, we sat silently and watched the kids playing.

"Those kids are healthy. They can get on with the business of being children without the terror of..." She paused. "This is what I've done as Lady Provost."

Then, with surprising voice, she called, "CAILLEN! FRASER! COME."

Two children split off from their pals and came running.

The girl, clearly the older sister of Dallin who I'd met earlier – same riot of carrot red hair, same devil-may-care smile, but her mother's green eyes – asked, "Ay Mum?"

"Thomas, I'd like you to meet Caillen."

I awkwardly slipped down from the hay wagon, faced the young girl, and extended my hand, which she shook with surprising firmness. "It's my pleasure to meet you. I'm Thomas."

She smiled.

From the wagon, Barbara said, "And that young man is Fraser, Fraser MacDonald."

A chill ran up my spine.

Again, I extended my hand. "Nice to meet you. I'm Thomas, Thomas MacDonald."

The boy's face broke into one of those smiles that goes all the way to the eyes.

"Which clan?"

I just shook my head. "I...I don't know."

Barbara said, "You two go play. And Caillen, not too rough."

They turned and ran back to their game.

As I watched them go, Barbara said, "You have just met the future Queen of Scotland, and Fraser, he will be the greatest engineer our land ever produced. And of course, they are your ancestors."

My knees felt weak. I turned and faced her. "How do you know...?"

She laughed and held her kicking belly. "Surely, you don't think you are the only one who uses time travel?"

I grabbed onto the wagon to keep from collapsing.

She laughed again. "Maybe you better get back up here. Looks like you need to sit down."

With all the grace of a zombie, I pulled myself back up and lay back in the hay.

Barbara, watching the kids at play, said, "And now, we address why you are here. You ponder your future, wondering if you will amount to anything of value. Recently, you have fallen in love with a woman who your heart will not tolerate losing, especially because you question if you are worthy of her. You have had failures in your life so far. You wonder who you really are. Correct?"

Again, I was speechless.

"Thomas, listen to my words. You have my blood and that of my worthless brother in your body. You must choose which blood will lead you. You must choose. No one can choose for you. But be aware; that red headed girl out there and her ruffian friend who will someday be a fine handsome man and will cherish her, together, they will lead Scotland out of its plague-infested existence, to a place where children can grow up to be great. Their blood is in your body as well. The choice is yours."

I sat up and stared into her intense green eyes.

The breeze had become steady and strong.

She shifted. "And now, I think I need my midwife."

# TEN

Waking up early without an alarm clock had become a welcome habit. I lay in my king-size bed thinking about my ancestral visit to Scotland, no longer questioning my time travels but rather examining what I had learned. Smelling a bit like barnyard residue made me want to take a shower, but that could wait until I got back from my run through the greenway. "Push for four miles, Laddie!" I told myself. The sun welcomed my efforts as we greeted the day together, and I raced against its full rise and another warm fall day.

Invigorated by my cleansing shower, I grabbed a fresh pair of jeans and pulled on one of my new button-down shirts. Boat shoes without socks finished my new look and I checked the mirror to see the reflection I hoped Cherie would like. She looked so gorgeous at the library the other day, so put together in her black pinstriped suit and ruffly pink blouse. She nearly took my breath away. Her elegantly long legs caught me off guard. I'd only seen her in casual clothes. But this last time, after our thwarted date, really made me wonder how I could stay in her life, why she would want me around. I had to keep reminding myself to be positive.

I decided to get my kitchen prep-ready before heading to work. I have so many barely used pots, pans and utensils, it's laughable. The fancy stainless steel spice rack will definitely come in handy for tonight's dinner and will look nice sitting out on the counter instead of stuffed in the pantry. Funny, these kitchen supplies are the only things I kept of my mother's, even though she hardly ever used them. These cookie cutters can stay in the bottom drawer, I sighed, remembering—

"Mom, can't we make some Christmas cookies? My sixth-grade English class is doing research on holiday foods used in fiction we've been reading. We could use this candy cane cutter and decorate cookies in striped icing and..."

"Oh, Thomas. Don't be silly. You know I don't have time for that. This is a very busy time for me, trying to get sales trips in before the holidays. I'll add 'cookies' to this list for your father. You know, having a career and staying on top requires sacrifices, right? You'll learn that when you start a career."

"Not everybody wants a career, Mom. Some people are happy just having a job and raising a family. You know?"

I can laugh now, but the look on my mother's face when I made that obtuse observation almost killed me. It did kill her. She ignored her cancer symptoms too long, pursuing her glorious career. Guess I got the last laugh.

Satisfied that I'd done all I could to ready my apartment for dinner with Cherie, I closed the door. I still had time for a decent meal before work.

Breakfast at Lulu's Diner satisfied my immediate need—food. This exercise thing has spiked my appetite for more than OJ in a plastic cup and an egg biscuit from my formerly favorite drive-throughs.

"My, oh, my. Look at you, Thomas! All gussied up! Are you meeting your girlfriend this morning?"

"What? Who? No, I'm just ready for a busy day at the bookstore and—"

"Thomas, don't you let that pretty little girl get away. She was eating up your every word and looking like you were the only person in the room."

"Who? Oh, that was just a customer. I hardly know her. Uh, I'll have blueberry waffles, a fruit cup and a side order of bacon. And coffee, of course."

"Got it." Lulu winked and patted me on my wrist.

As a matter of fact, I wanted to tell Lulu, her name is Cherie Abernathy, and we have a date tonight. She called me when she finally broke away from her work at the library and asked for a raincheck. But I kept it to myself, afraid my joy would burst if I told anyone.

I paid my bill and walked two doors down to the bookstore. My plan for the day was to put up the new posters Horace had brought back from the last concert he attended, then explore the best side dish options for boeuf bourguignon. There are definitely advantages to working here and reading on the job topped the list. "Hmmm, mashed potatoes or noodles? What would she prefer, Meow?"

The bell over the door tinkled. "Excuse me." An elderly gentleman approached, as if looking for someone. "Oh. Good morning. I thought you were talking to someone. Didn't want to interrupt."

"No sir. Well, just talking to myself, I guess. Actually, talking to the cat here. Our resident rodent protection system. Name's Meow. Original, huh?"

"Not a bad idea, young man. A listener that doesn't talk back. Well, anyway. I'm looking for your historical fiction section. Do you have the books sorted by genre, or—"

"Yes! Yes, we do. We do now. Follow me and I'll show you where they start. Anything in particular you're looking for?"

"I just finished *Outlander*. Rather enjoy the Scottish setting, but that's probably too specific for you. I can just browse here, if that's alright. This place seems more organized than I remember it."

"Of course. Look around. I just finished *The Other Queen*. Fascinating story."

The man stood tall and hooked his cane on the shelf. "My, my. A bookstore where the help actually reads. How long have you been working here?"

"Almost seven years. Bounced around in retail and then waited on tables for a while, but this really suits me. I've always liked to read and just recently decided to reorganize this place. *Learning is the only thing the mind never exhausts.* Even a new and used bookstore needs some order, some symmetry. Glad you noticed the changes."

"Been coming in here for years. Don't recall seeing you before. I'll take this one at your recommendation and I'll look around a bit more."

I took *The Other Queen* from him. "I'll hold it at the register. Take your time browsing."

The phone rang. My cell, not the store. It's Cherie. "Take your time, sir." Don't panic, Thomas. Where'sm yphonewhere'smyphonewhere's... . "Hello?" Her voice so full of life, so lovely, so deep and sincere. "Okay.

That sounds great. Red wine and French bread will balance the meal out perfectly. I'll see you at seven thirty. And don't hesitate to call if you can't find it when you get in the parking lot. Call me and I can come down to meet you, help you carry your things up. I am on the third floor, you know." Stupid of me to think she can't find my apartment. Stupid of me to suggest the accomplished hiker can't make it up three flights of steps. Stupid. "I should have asked if she liked potatoes or noodles."

"Meow," the cat stretched.

"I'll take these three books for now. Ring me up. Son? You alright? Is it a girl?"

"I'm fine. No, Meow is a boy. Thanks for coming in. Come back soon."

He turned when he reached the door. "Son, if she called you it means she likes you. Feed her what you like. She'll love it. Have a good day...and a good night."

"Meow, remind me to pick up some potatoes for tonight."

The shop stayed fairly busy for the remainder of the day. I couldn't flip the CLOSED sign fast enough, stopped for potatoes and some eclairs, and hurried home. I had two and a half hours to prep, shower, and set the table.

The kitchen smelled delicious until the phone startled my confidence. "She's not coming. I'll put on some music to make it seem like I'm relaxed, chill." I walked toward the balcony and looked down. "Hello? Yes, yes I see you. Come on up." I turned the music down a few decibels and opened the door.

"Dinner was five-star, Thomas. What a wonderful

way to end a workday. I could get used to this. My place next time, but your cooking puts me to shame. Do you like Chinese?" Cherie's hearty laugh always caught me off guard. Her turquoise sweatshirt sported some sparkles around the neck, drawing me to those gem-like eyes.

We cleaned off the table and easily loaded the dish-washer, as if it were second nature. I could get used to this, too, I wanted to say. Instead, I put four eclairs on a plate and carried the rest of our wine onto the balcony. "I do like Chinese. And Mexican. And Italian. And even American. Think it's too cool out here?"

"It's perfect. The view is great up here. Do you have coffee?" She curled her legs up on the not-too-comfort-able sofa I kept outside.

I put on a pot of coffee, turned up the music, and sat as close to her as I dared. "So, you never did tell me how your hiking weekend went with your friend. Did you have fun?"

Her joyful voice played from one adventure to the other, but I hardly listened, couldn't stop staring at her full lips, wanting to touch her cheekbones, let her hair down. Instead, "Coffee might be ready. No cream, no sugar, right?"

"You remembered. You are the best."

Maybe I am, maybe I am. I put two hot mugs on the small metal table and picked up an éclair. "Oh, sorry. Do you want a fork? You probably need a fork." I start-ed to get up, but Cherie grabbed my hand and pulled me back down.

"Watch this." She picked up the chocolate éclair with two fingers and took a generous bite. "This is the proper way to eat an éclair, Thomas." Again, the laugh.

I wiped some cream filling off of her nose and stayed close. We kissed and she tasted delicious. She kissed me back and we let the coffee get cold. I fed her the rest of my éclair and she stuffed the last of hers in my mouth. The outdoor sofa grew more uncomfortable, but I didn't want to move, afraid to break the spell. We touched each other and I longed for more.

"Thomas." She interrupted the flow. "This is such a perfect night. I don't want to spoil it. I just...it's just... I'm so—"

I stood immediately. "Sorry, sorry. I understand. You probably still aren't over that schmuck you almost married up in Boston. The most proper Harvard graduate with the pompous parents and the law firm and the bow ties and the Porsche. I'll bet he would never approve of eating an éclair without a sterling silver fork. What was his name? Prentice? Preston?" My outburst surprised me and I think it scared her. Shit. I just ruined everything.

"Sit down, Thomas. I am so over Phillipe. That's why I moved back down here. Fresh start. I like you a lot, but I don't want to rush you. You were hurting when we found each other. That silly waste of air, Stacy was her name, right? She had no sympathy at all after your father died, just when you needed someone. I'm so glad she dumped you. She was worthless. I'm so glad we found each other Thomas. That's what I was going to say, before you so RUDELY interrupted me." Then she laughed, a song I loved to hear. "I need to use the restroom. Be right back."

I inhaled the onion aromas still penetrating my place, gathered up the mugs and turned the lights down in the living room.

She had let her hair down and came out hugging

herself. "I love that song. *'Shower the people you love with love, show them the way that you feel, things are gonna be much better if you only will...'* You like James Taylor?"

"I'll admit I like to listen to him sometimes. Throwback. My Dad liked him."

"Well, at least you knew your Dad. Sounds like he loved your mother and just...lost it when she died so suddenly. People deal with things differently. It helps to talk about it." She returned the remaining eclairs to the refrigerator, put her arms around me and hugged my soul, patting my back, combing her fingers through my hair. "I'm here for the long haul, Thomas. Thomas the doubter. Don't doubt me." She smiled, we kissed.

"I love...your hair down. You usually wear it pulled back or up or—"

"Oh, since we're changing the subject, I have a question for you. What's with all those suitcases at the foot of your bed? Couldn't help but notice them. You aren't planning to skip out on me are you?" She poked my chest, tilted her head, and looked right into my eyes. "Hmmm?"

"No, Cherie. No, my dear," I dared to say. "That is such a long story. A story I doubt you would believe. But how about I tell you about their magic the next time we get together? Your place with Chinese takeout?"

I walked her to her car and watched until the taillights disappeared around the corner. "Solid." I stood there in the crisp fall air feeling complete, like a real person. "I think I'm going to make it."

I turned off all the lights but left the music playing, tapping small-medium-large with an unexpected passion. I was unafraid of the future or the past.

Before I opened my eyes, I sensed it had happened again, transported to a different place and time. I lay there trying to imagine what century I would find myself in, what country, what wise and famous person I would meet next. Clueless, I opened my eyes to find myself in a college dorm, lying on a twin bed in the middle of the afternoon. Since no one came to greet me or rouse me out of my stupor or welcome me to a fantasy world, I got myself up and looked out the window. "You have got to be kidding me," I said to no one. "Back in Chapel Hill? Really? I'm outta here."

My walk across the quad did not conjure up fond memories, and all I wanted to do was figure out how to get back to Charlotte without running in to anyone I knew, but the more I walked, the less familiar things felt. I saw protest signs, never an unusual sight, but these were against the Vietnam War. I was relieved that it was far enough back in time that I would not see anyone from my few years here. I sat on a bench to think.

"Hey, there, Thomas. I've been looking for you. Wishing you were back on campus?" He removed a Boston Red Sox cap from his head and smiled.

"Not at all. Not here anyway." I tried to place the very bald, denim-clad man. "Who are you and why am I here?" He stared me down and broke out in a big smile.

"I knew your Dad."

My silence could outwait his. He brought me here, so he could stir up the past. I put my elbows on my knees and looked away.

"Mind if I sit down?"

"Free country." I moved to the far end of the bench.

"Your father was my earliest fan. We roomed together when I first started writing songs. He encouraged me to follow my dreams and be my own person."

"Good for him." I looked at the man then, squaring up his age. Seemed to be around the same age Dad would have been now. So. I was plopped down in the middle of the 1960's but the guy who brought me here seemed to have come from my present. This was a new twist.

"You are at a crossroads right now, Thomas. The direction you take is completely up to you. Your friend Socrates said, 'Know thyself.' Will you move forward or be sucked down in your own despair?"

Game on, I decided. This would be over soon, so I may as well move things along. "You sound familiar. Have we ever met?"

"No, Thomas. I met your father in Boston, back in the early 60's. We roomed together in a psych hospital, where neither of us wanted to be. I wanted to sing and Shamus wanted to paint, but our parents thought we were both nuts. Just before I was released to form a band with my brother Alex, Shamus encouraged me to keep writing songs. *Musicians are the mouthpieces of humanity.* He told me that, and I stole his words. Say it all the time."

"Are you—you're James Taylor? I never knew my father knew you. Oh my God. He always loved your music, played it all the time, but he never said a word about knowing you. You're kidding, right? You've got to be kidding." I stood up and walked in front of him, both hands on my head.

"Yep. Shamus was ashamed of being diagnosed with depression. It kept him out of the military, but he told everybody he had flat feet. Went on to become a pretty damn good chemical engineer. Smart, smart guy, but could never admit his weakness. Me, I just dove into music and drugs and alcohol and bounced around on highs and lows for years. Shamus, he dealt with his problems by marrying your Mom and putting her on a pedestal. She could do no wrong, and when she got sick he fell apart."

"Yeah, well, you're still here and he isn't, so I'd say you made better choices."

"Thomas, we are here today because I want to re-pay your Dad's kindness. Yes, I am one of America's best-selling music artists of all time, was inducted into the Rock and Roll Hall of Fame almost ten years ago. But, man oh man, did I ever screw up my personal life for years and years and years. Married Carly way too young. Nearly died of alcohol and drug abuse."

"O.K. What has this got to do with me? I have no addictions and I can't sing. Why are we here? Did you go here?"

"No, Thomas. To my parents' distress, I spent my college fund trying to become a singer."

"Good choice. You succeeded. So, I repeat, what has your success got to do with me? I'm a college dropout who is definitely not a success."

"You've met someone, Thomas. Embrace this awe-some luck. You probably didn't know that my father taught here."

"And...?"

"He was the Dean of the Medical School here. Isaac Taylor. Brilliant. Successful. And an alcoholic who committed suicide. Like your father. They left us hanging, left us feeling incomplete. Don't take as long as it took me to get your priorities straight, Thomas. *Shower the people you love with love*, Thomas. It's as simple as that."

We walked across the campus, winding our way around the protestors and the flower child images, and James told me of the intermittent communications he had with my Dad. "After he married your Mom, I thought he finally found himself. Never heard from him again. Not until your Mom died. He reached out to me to talk about my song 'Fire and Rain,' but I was between gigs and just let the conversation go. Wish I hadn't."

We circled back to the dorm where I started and shook hands. I climbed the stairs, glad to see my baggage waiting for me. It seemed smaller somehow, and I lay down hoping to get back home soon, anxious to tell Cherie how much she means to me. I needed to figure out how to tell her about my incredible adventures, being transported into the past, without sounding like a total nutcase. I cannot lose this love that I've found.

*I've seen fire and I've seen rain.*
*I've seen sunny days that I thought would never end.*
*I've seen lonely times when I could not find a friend,*
*But I always thought that I'd see you again.*

# ELEVEN

A little after noon the next day, I was in the back room unpacking yet another shipment of books Horace had sent when the bell over the door jangled.

"Thomas?" that familiar voice said, and I jumped up and ran toward the front of the store, tripping over a box and almost upending myself.

I managed to compose myself and said in my most calm voice, "Cherie, I wasn't expecting you. What a pleasant surprise!" I hesitated. "Hey, it's lunch time. Want to try Lulu's?"

"I'd really love to, Thomas, but I only have a few minutes. I have some bad news and I wanted to deliver it in person. I'm afraid I'm going to have to call off dinner tonight."

My heart sank. Of course. I knew it was too good to be true.

"My cousin Ruth-Ann, whom I haven't seen in years and was never particularly fond of, suddenly remembered she had cousin in Charlotte when she was coming here for some kind of conference. And how convenient – maybe she could stay with me – just for five nights. She would be busy during the day and maybe into the evening. She wouldn't put me out at all. What could I say? She's family. Sooo, I'm afraid dinner at my place is not going to happen for a while."

My shoulders sagged and those negative voices started chattering, but then I had a vision of the host of people I had recently visited, all saying, "You can do it. You are worth it."

"That's a bummer, but we can do my place again – something simple this time. I looked at her and smiled confidently.

She smiled back. "Sounds good, but then I owe you big time. See you tonight. 7:30 again?

She left and I soared through the rest of my day.

When I got home, I set about straightening up the apartment. I wanted everything to be just right. I went into the bedroom, hopeful that another stellar meal, a little James Taylor playing softly in the background, and some cuddling on the couch could eventually lead here. Just in case, I changed the sheets, long past their expiration date, and put clean towels in the bathroom, fantasizing about Cherie emerging from the shower, blonde hair dripping, shimmering wet body wrapped, more or less in the bath towel. A fantasy? Perhaps. But if I had learned nothing else lately, it was that it was important to dream big.

I had become so accustomed to nimbly dodging the suitcases, careful not to inadvertently send myself off on a journey through time and space, that I hardly noticed how much space they took up. This could be a problem with someone new to the room. They wouldn't fit in my closet, and there was precious little extra space in the room, except for a small nook in the corner by the bathroom. I gingerly wheeled them over, feeling the accustomed tingling and hoping mightily that they wouldn't do their thing tonight. If they did, would Cherie automatically come with me? Or would she be left staring at an empty space beside her when she woke up?

They weren't completely out of the way, but it was better. Maybe I'd just drape a shirt over them and they wouldn't be so obvious. She had asked about them last time, and I knew I would have to tell her about them, but not now, not tonight.

The evening was going splendidly. Cherie not only laughed when I said *I love cooking with wine. Sometimes I even put it in the food,* she said, "Don't think you can fool me Thomas MacDonald. I know a Julia Child line when I hear one." That precipitated a spirited conversation about the great kooky chef, whom she loved, to which I was able to add a few little-known bits of information.

As we sipped some chardonnay and ate our chicken casserole, I tried to steer the conversation to topics where I had some personal experience and could impress her with the depth and breadth of my knowledge. Turns out she wasn't much of a Conrad fan but she loved Dickens, and I surprised her with my vivid detail of Dickens' London. And I knew that at least her nephew was a big hockey fan, so we spent a good bit of time talking about the Canadians.

"This may sound corny," she said as we finished up our last bites, "but one thing I love about you is that you're such a great conversationalist. You know so much about such a variety of topics. Most men I meet are stuck on sports or themselves and the latest big deal they pulled off."

I said a silent thank you to all my mentors and said,

"I believe there are two eclairs left in the fridge and I have the coffee ready to go."

As we sat on the couch, coffee and eclairs at the ready, I took the lead. "I have been told by an expert that this is how to eat an éclair." I bit slowly into the creamy delicacy, never taking my eyes off her, and let it melt in my mouth as I drew closer to her. Our kiss was slow and gentle at first, but then we both gave in to feelings that had been pretty well checked until now.

"I know you were hesitant last time – afraid that maybe I was still hurting, rebounding, but I assure you," I said, as my hands wandered, "you are the only one . . ." The rest of the sentence was lost in a flurry of kisses.

"Oh Thomas," she said giggling. "I do believe you have managed to persuade . . ." she kissed me softly, "a willing . . ." another kiss, "partner. But this partner needs to go to the bathroom. Don't go away. I'll be right back." She kissed me again and then went through the bedroom into the bathroom.

"Okay, Thomas," she said when she came back. "Why did you try to hide those suitcases under your shirts? I think we need to have a conversation."

Oh no. Not now. "Cherie, please. I'll tell you all about it later. Let's not let it spoil the evening."

I tried moving close to her and recapturing the moments before she went into the bedroom, but she was having none of it. "I just don't understand why you get so weird every time I mention those silly suitcases."

Oh shit. This wasn't the way I had planned it at all. "Okay. Cherie, please sit down and I'll explain everything."

"I certainly hope so."

"Well, you know how I talked about Dickens and Julia Child and Ken and all those other people?"

"Yeah. But what do they have to do with the suitcases?"

"Well, um see . . ." I was stumbling. My trips were wonderful and fantastical and very real to me, but making someone else believe in them was not easy. "These suitcases, they have these special powers." I was definitely getting the 'are you shitting me?' look. "I mean, I'm still not sure exactly how it works, but when I touch them, I get a tingly feeling, and somehow, after I go to sleep, I wake up in these amazing places, like Greece and London, and meet people like Leonardo and Dickens."

"Thomas, do you realize how crazy this sounds? Who are you? I have spent the evening with a wonderful conversationalist who has educated himself on a wide variety of subjects, and all of a sudden I'm talking to a mentally deranged kook who's talking about suitcases that whoosh him off through space and time and just happen to hook him up with famous people. What have you been smoking?"

Her look of confusion and utter disbelief left me completely disheartened. "Oh, damn, Cherie. This is why I didn't tell you earlier. I know it sounds crazy, but please let me explain.

"Okay," she said, "I certainly hope you can make sense of this whole thing."

"See, I found these suitcases out by the trash bin a couple of weeks ago and I brought them home and put them in here, and when I happened to touch them, I got this tingling feeling, but I ignored it and went to bed. The next thing I knew, I woke up in Florence and met

Leonardo and he took me to his studio and explained all about the Vitruvian man and it was so exciting. The whole thing was just mind blowing."

"Thomas, 'mind blowing' is the most sensible thing you have said lately. This is scary. Time travel is stuff you read about or watch on TV. It's not real. These people you say you visited, they're not real. This whole thing is . . .

"Cherie," I interrupted, "Please listen to me."

"Thomas, I'm really concerned about you. I'm going to give you the name of someone you can talk to about all of this stuff. She's really helped me. You've told me about the problems you had after your mother died and then after your father committed suicide. I think you have some issues that need to be resolved, and they're manifesting themselves in this weird way. I care about you, I really do, and the best thing I can do is to make sure you talk to somebody who can help you sort fact from fiction. Please call Dr. Ratkiewitz. She'll help you get yourself straightened out. When our parents are snatched away from us, as has happened to both of us, we carry a lot of unresolved feelings. Mine weren't like this, but they were real – and complicated. Believe me, she can help. Then, after you have spoken to her, let me know and then we can get back together." She went into the living room, pulled a card out of her purse and handed it to me. She hesitated for a moment, looked longingly at me, and said, "Please call her, Thomas," and then she walked out.

I sat on the edge of the bed and for the first time since my father died, I wept long and hard. I loved her as I had never loved anyone else in my life. I loved her laughter, her wit, her sparkling conversation, and the way she made me feel important and special. Because of her, I finally felt truly alive. And now it was gone, all because of those stupid suitcases. I got up and gave them a hearty kick. "Take that, you bloody pieces of shit! Why don't you just take me away? Far away! And don't bother bringing me back."

They did not take me away, and I eventually did crawl out of bed and wandered into the bookstore, accompanied now by the old Thomas, who taunted me: *Did you really think she could fall for you? She's way out of your league, man. Give it up!*

But I wouldn't give it up. I couldn't. I called her repeatedly and left messages on her voice mail. I texted and emailed. She texted back once: "I miss you too, but my doctor friend says you haven't called. PLEASE CALL HER! When you do, then we can get back together."
I thought briefly, " Okay. If that's what it will take, I can give her a call." But then I realized that she wouldn't believe me any more than Cherie – or any sane person would - because it does sound like the story of somebody totally unhinged. And for a few moments, I started questioning myself: could it all have been a dream? No! I knew it was real, but how could I convince anyone else?
One day, almost a week later, I was sitting amid several stacks of unshelved books, playing James Taylor over and over again, the words of *Fire and Rain* seared into my brain:

*I've seen fire and I've seen rain.*
*I've seen sunny days that I thought would never end.*

*I've seen lonely times when I could not find a friend,*
*But I always thought that I'd see you again.*

I *would* see her again - I just needed to figure out
a way to prove that I really could travel back in time.
Then I got an idea. I remember Horace telling me that
when he bought the bookstore, the owner said it had
been quite the gathering place for counter-culture fol-
lowers during the 50s and 60s – beatniks and hippies
found a home there. Though far from the Greenwich
Village and San Francisco, the BookWorm somehow
gained a reputation, and many authors and poets
came to speak, like Alan Ginsberg, who gave a reading of *Howl!* and Timothy Leary who supposedly had
dropped in on his way to dropping out, though that
story was suspect. And on any given evening, the literary elite, such as they were, would gather to read and
discuss works like *Naked Lunch* and *Dharma Bums,*
and, it was hinted, smoke a good bit of weed.

Maybe if I could travel back to that period, I could
bring back something or show her something that
would erase all her doubts. I had given up on digital
media and sat down to write a letter. After several false
starts, I finally settled on the following:

*Dear Cherie,*

*I cannot tell you how much I miss your brilliant
smile, your sparkling personality, your stimulat-
ing conversation, and your warm embrace. You
made me come alive; you made me believe in myself. With you gone, I feel as if my heart has been
ripped out and left to rot on a trash heap.*

*I know the suitcase story is hard to believe — I didn't believe it myself at first. It seemed too weird, as if I had entered the Twilight Zone. But I swear to you, it is real.*

*If you will please come by the bookstore, I think I have a way to prove it to you. If I don't succeed, you can walk out and never see me again. But if I do, and if you choose, we can set off together on some of the most amazing experiences of a lifetime.*

*If you miss me even a fraction as much as I miss you, I hope you will give me one last chance.*

*Love, Thomas*

I mailed the letter, and then I watched and I waited. I looked up and down the street outside the bookstore several times a day, and I checked my mailbox when I got home at night and again when I left in the morning. In the meantime, I tried to stick to my exercise regimen, though I did it without the old enthusiasm. If she said yes, I wanted to be in peak performance mode.

Then, four days later, at 5:02 PM, the bell rang, and in she walked.

"Thomas?" she called, a bit timidly.

I had to rein myself in to keep from running up to her and sweeping her into my arms. We stood for a moment, not saying anything. Then she said, "I missed you."

And there, in between Science Fiction and Romance, we embraced and shared a kiss that registered somewhere between PG and X+.

When she finally pulled away – I was ready to keep going right then and there – she said, gasping a bit, "Okay, let's just take a breath here. As hard as I try, I can't believe that the wonderful man I know and lo . . . like a lot could suddenly turn into a kook who believes in travelling suitcases. So somehow, despite all reason and logic, maybe there's something to it. You did have some pretty unique details about Julia and Dickens and Ken and a whole lot of other subjects you managed to lead us to. And if it is true? Holy shit. That would be insane!. But for now, I eagerly await the proof you promised, and I really hope you can show it to me."

With that, she smiled and walked slowly out the door, looking back at me several times.

I couldn't close up fast enough. I raced home, stopping for take-out on the way, chanting "BookWorm in the 50s and 60s" over and over again. I was still a little fuzzy on how the suitcases decided exactly where to send me, but I planned to do everything in my power to get back there and find something, anything that would prove to Cherie that the suitcases were real and that we had a lifetime of adventures of ahead of us.

As I waited for time to pass, I finished up the second bottle of wine from last night and read up as much as I could on the Beatniks and Hippies and that whole movement that I had heard so much about. Then I lay down and hoped and prayed that the suitcases would not let me down.

I woke up in a place that seemed at once familiar and strange. The bookcases that line the walls today were there, but the interior of the room was re-configured. Instead of carefully labeled rows of bookcases, there was a great open space with a podium at one end.

"Thomas, thank goodness you're here – just in time to help me set up."

A tall man - bearded, long-haired, about my age - was bustling about setting up chairs. "If you'll take over with these chairs, I can get the coffee and 'brownies'" – he gave me a wink – "ready. I'm Lawrence, by the way. Not Ferlinghetti, alas, but Arnold."

"Pleased to meet you, Lawrence," was the extent of our conversation. He was obviously not taking time out for pleasantries. I thought I did a pretty good job, squeezing about 30 chairs into a confined space, but it wasn't quite what Lawrence had envisioned, so he straightened them up a bit.

"There!" he sighed. "Wish we could get more in here. When we have a special guest like tonight, people are going to be searching for any scrap of floor to perch on."

"Special guest?" I asked. "Who's coming."

"Sorry. Of course you wouldn't know. It's Allen Ginsberg. He's coming to do a special reading of his amazing poem *Howl!* We had to move heaven and earth to get him here. And I'm so eager to make a good impression. A couple of our local boys are going to be reading first. I had my dealer get me an extra supply of weed so the atmosphere will be perfect."

At that last bit of information, my mouth dropped

open, but Lawrence didn't notice; he had moved on to rearranging his brownies. This was definitely his night to shine.

"Thomas, would you mind getting a couple of bags out of the wall safe?"

The wall safe? What wall safe? Lawrence noticed my befuddlement.

"Don't you know about the wall safe?"

He went over to the bookshelf on the far wall, removed a couple of books, pushed something, and a section of two shelves about two feet long slid open. "The Charlotte constabulary frowns on weed – and just about everything else that makes life enjoyable. They've raided us a couple of times and get furious when they can't find anything."

"Aha!" I thought. "This might be the proof I need – a secret space in the wall, a little weed." A good beginning, but I would need more than that.

People started drifting in, sparking a party atmosphere aided by freely dispensed weed and special brownies. Lawrence, however, was more anxious than ever. His special guest had yet to arrive. The two local poets read to an enthusiastic crowd. And then they read a few more poems, this time to a crowd that was growing considerably less enthusiastic. And then, a car pulled up outside, and a bespectacled man with a full beard and wild fringe of hair stepped through the door, greeted by cheers.

He stood up at the podium and began: *I saw the best minds of my generation destroyed by madness starving hysterical naked, dragging themselves through the negro streets at dawn looking for an angry fix . . .* I had read the poem last night, but as he stood there intoning the living nightmare he saw around him, the poem hammered away at my soul. Poetry had never been my thing, but he opened up a whole new world to me.

As he read, Lawrence was busy with his Polaroid, snapping photos of Ginsberg and the enthralled crowd – great publicity for the BookWorm. I had forgotten about those marvels of instant developing popular back in the 60s. But now I knew I could give Cherie the proof she wanted.

As the crowd that thronged around him gradually dissipated, I approached him with my new copy of *Howl!* "That was wonderful, Mr. Ginsberg," I stammered. "Would you mind autographing this and inscribing it to Cherie? And Lawrence, could you please take a picture of me with Mr. Ginsberg?

As soon as I woke up, I texted Cherie: *I got the proof. Can't wait till you see it. Much love.*

I arrived at the store early, carefully placing my autographed copy of *Howl!* and the Polaroid photo of me with Alan Ginsberg on the counter, and started to search for the special bookcase. Since things had changed quite a bit since the '50s, it took me a while to find the exact spot. Holding my breath, I pushed the books aside, reached back and pushed. Voila! There was the secret cache. I reached in and pulled out a bag that disintegrated in my hand. This should convince even the most hardened skeptic.

I tried to keep busy all morning, organizing and rearranging, but I couldn't concentrate. When I realized that I had placed a biography of Winston Churchill in

Science Fiction, I laughed – yes, I laughed. I didn't beat myself up – and kept on going. Anything to make the time pass.

A little after noon, Cherie walked in. I ran to her and was so excited to show her my evidence that I didn't even take time to give her a kiss.

"Look," I said, holding up a signed copy of *Howl!* " I had Alan Ginsberg dedicate it to you."

"Wait, wait, wait . . ." Cherie said. "I don't know what on earth you're talking about."

"Sorry," I said, "of course you don't. Let me explain." I told her the story of the incredible evening. "And look, here's a picture – remember those old Polaroids our parents took? – it's of me with Alan Ginsberg. And, the piece de resistance" - I walked over to the bookcase and opened it up – "the wall safe with a little residue of the stuff that kept them flying high."

"Oh my God," Cherie said, looking at me with astonishment and delight. "This is crazy . . . nutso. . .bonkers. But Holy shit! It's real! You really can travel through time! I need some time to wrap my head around this."

"And guess what," I said, grasping her shoulders and looking straight into her eyes, "we can do it together."

She laughed, I laughed, and then we had one long, marvelous kiss.

# TWELVE

"**N**ow listen," Cherie said, "tonight, you keep your hand off your wallet. This is my treat."

We took a table for two in Filho's Cucina, over by the window with the view of the rain-washed courtyard. The waiter delivered menus, filled our water glasses, and promised to be back shortly. The restaurant was packed, noisy, and smelled of garlic and onions.

Cherie reached across the table and squeezed my hand. "This makes up for me standing you up that evening when my cousin plopped herself in my apartment."

"Unnecessary but fine," I said. "That's a deal."

"This is my favorite restaurant. I love the food here. And now," Cherie said, "would you mind if I ordered for us both?"

I tossed the menu aside. "Lead on McDuff. I am in your capable hands. Order away."

When the waiter returned, Cherie ordered an antipasto for two and a large Caesar salad for starters, and then for our main courses, gemelli con polo and ravioli di aragosta. And of course, a bottle of Ruffino Chianti Classico Riserva.

The waiter smiled, said, "molto bene," and hurried off.

Moments later, we were locking eyes and toasting to 'us.'

She lowered her glass, looked both ways to insure no one was eaves dropping, then leaned across the table. In a voice hardly more than a whisper, she said, "I need to ask you about that autographed copy of *Howl!* and the picture of you and Ginsberg you gave to me. Now," Cherie paused, searched for the right words, then blurted out, "It's like this...my heart believes the story you've told me, but my head is struggling. Does that make sense to you?"

I leaned in co-conspiratorially. "Boy oh boy, do I ever understand what you're saying. I've been doing this time travel thing for a while now and my brain still doesn't believe it. But I swear, it's real." I snapped my fingers. "And I almost forgot," I pulled out my wallet and within, took out two tickers to a Boston Bruins vs Montreal Canadians playoff game from thirty-two years ago.

"And, in case that's not enough, I have these. Take a look."

Cherie studied the tickets and furrowed her brow. "What are these?"

"In one of my travels, I went back to Montreal for well, a long story. But in that adventure, I was given two tickets to a game that I never used. Check out the dates on those tickets."

She did.

"Only a crazy person would have tickets to a playoff game and not use them! The street value prior to the game was out of sight, but now, those are worth a fortune. To a collector of sports memorabilia, those would be like a mint set of 1921 Peace Silver Dollar coins, or a block of uncancelled Inverted Jenny twenty-four cent stamps. But that's not why I still have them. I had no intention of collecting them. I would have loved to see that game. The reason I didn't use them was because I came back from the past to the present before the game was played. Follow?"

"Maybe."

We fell silent and she held me with her cobalt blue eyes. Then she smiled. "This travel thing, I think I actually believe you."

Taking a deep breath, I continued. "Furthermore, I think I've figured out a way we can travel together."

She leaned back in her chair and studied me. "Oh?"

"Look, let's back up. Let me start again." I stared at my wine. "If you could travel back in time, anywhere, anytime, where would you want to go?"

A smile began to grow from her lips. She lowered her eyes. "I know this sounds corny, but I think I'd like to go back to Paris in 1922 during the Hemingway and Fitzgeralds and Gertrude Stein time. Just to see if it was as glorious as it is portrayed in that movie..."

*"Midnight in Paris?"*

"Yes!" she exclaimed. "I love that movie!"

I could feel my heart pounding. "Me too. It's my favorite 'go to' flick."

Cherie took a healthy swallow of chianti. "I think that's where I'd like to go. And you know, I would have loved to live there back then." She paused and studied her wine. "Life was simpler. And let me tell you a secret. I believe I have some talent, buried way deep down, that could have surfaced if allowed. Being with all the artists and writers, I think that may have done it for me."

"Wow," I said. "I've had some of those the very same thoughts. One of my dreams is giving writing a go. I've dabbled with it a few times but never hung in there and actually completed something. I think I could. And I think I've got a novel or two inside. More than once, I've read a New York Times bestseller and said, *I could do that!* Just like you, I'd welcome the chance." I sipped my wine. "Everything I've read about Paris in the 20's appeals to me. Living there? I'd love to give it a go."

Cherie leaned close. "Do you think we can take that time travel suitcase of yours there?"

I nodded my head. "I believe we can make that happen."

As we entered my apartment, I took Cherie by the hand and pulled her close. "Are you okay with this?"

She hugged me. Tightly. For a long time. "I'm scared."

"Understandably. We can call the whole thing off."

"No. I want to give it a try."

"Okay."

I led her across my apartment to where the suitcases stood.

Looking into Cherie's eyes, I said, "Now we touch the suitcases. Like this."

I leaned over and rubbed the big piece, which yielded the now familiar tingle in my hands and faint ringing in my ears.

After a moment of hesitation, Cherie did the same. She stepped back. "What's with this tingling in my hands and..."

"Ringing in your ears. It's working."

She rubbed her hands. "What's next?"

"We sit on the couch and watch *Midnight in Paris*." We did.

When the movie was over and the credits were scrolling, Cherie asked, "And now what?"

"We go to bed."

"Oh?" she smiled coyly. "Is this part of the procedure?"

"Not usually," I smiled. "But I figured it was worth a try."

"I like how you think."

When I opened my eyes, I spotted Cherie, naked, outlined against an open window. She was staring out into a blanket of fog.

I propped myself up on an elbow, enjoying the scene. "You look lovely. What are you looking at?"

She turned to me, eyes wide, mouth agape. "I think it's the Seine! Can you believe it?"

"Actually, I can. And maybe you need to back away from the window before you attract a crowd."

Ignoring my comment, she pointed at the river. "We're really in Paris! I've just seen some old cars pass by below. And the people who are walking; they're dressed in old fashion clothing, just like in the movie!"

I slid out of bed and found my shirt. "Here. Put this on."

She did.

I joined her at the window. We were about two stories up. From what I could see, we were in some sort of boarding house. As the fog began to break up, the Eiffel Tower loomed ghost-like across the river.

"OH MY GOD!" she squealed, then squeezed me tighter than I thought possible.

"Let's get dressed and go see what the magic of Paris is all about."

For the next what, hour?, maybe two?, we strolled arm in arm, along the banks of the Seine. We crossed onto Ile de la Cite and sat in the gardens at Notre Dame. The flowers were dripping with diamonds of dew, many aflame in the dappled sunshine that was forcing its way through the fog. Then we walked some more. At the first outdoor café that smelled of coffee, we pulled up a chair.

In French, I ordered two croissants and two cups of café américain. When the waiter came with our food and drink, he smiled and in French asked, "Are you new to Paris?"

I said we were.

Then turning to Cherie, he asked, again in French, "How do you like our city so far?"

In perfect French, she said, "I love it. It's magical."

After the waiter departed, Cherie, wide-eyed, leaned across the table and whispered, "You're speaking French. I'm speaking French. And what's more, I understand what we're saying."

I laughed. "It seems to come with the turf. I'll explain later."

We were well into our food and hot drink, when suddenly, Cherie burst into tears.

I reached across the table and took her hand. "What's the matter?"

She wiped her eyes with the linen napkin. "I'm on overload. I just can't believe..."

Using my best comforting face, I asked, "Didn't you believe me?"

Now she laughed. "I thought I did but this really is Paris!"

I looked around. The fog was finally breaking up, allowing shafts of sunlight to lance down to the city. The Eiffel was framed by the brick buildings on either side of the cobblestone street. Vendors were setting up their kiosks. Women were sweeping the sidewalks with brooms. Men were laying out their papers on the newsstands. Paris was awakening.

A voice called out. "Thomas. Thomas! There you are. I've been expecting you. There are two matters we need to discuss right away." Without delay, a stocky woman came bustling up to our table. She had a decidedly round face and short cropped hair. Noticing I was not alone, she stated, "and you must be this Cherie I've been hearing about."

I jumped to my feet. "Of course, of course. Just like in the movie! You are Gertrude Stein! What a thrill to meet you. And this," I turned and looked into Cherie's eyes, "is my...my...my lover, Cherie."

Cherie smiled. It was the type of smile that approved of my choice of words.

Gertrude planted her hands to her hips. Brusquely, she turned toward Cherie and asked, "Are you American?"

Cherie blinked. "Yes."

"Writer?"

"No. Perhaps someday but for now, I'm working in a library as a historian."

"Do you speak French?"

Cherie nodded. "It seems as if I do."

"Good, good. That'll do nicely. Perfectly in fact." Gertrude signaled to a waiter who brought over a third chair and a pot of tea.

While this was taking place, Cherie tugged at my sleeve. Her eyes were wide. "I know I said this before, but I just don't get it: you're speaking French. I'm speaking French. And what's more, I understand what we're saying."

I laughed.

Gertrude got right into it. "Alice and I are throwing a party tonight for Picasso and Dali. They both just sold some of their paintings to a gallery in New York which is cause for celebration. The whole gang will be there: the Fitzgeralds, Hemingway, Luis Buñuel, Cole Porter, T.S. Elliot, Henri Matisse, all of them. Man Ray is coming with all his cameras to take pictures. You'll want to meet them all. We'll expect you both at eight. Don't be late."

Cherie whispered, "I have nothing to wear."

Gertrude, clearly anticipating such a predicament, dismissed the concern with a wave of her hand. "Not to worry. Alice bought a dress for you. It's hanging in your closet."

"Who's Alice?" Cherie asked.

I patted her arm. "Alice B Toklas. She and Gertrude are life partners." Then turning to Gertrude, I asked, "and what's this about our closet?"

It was Gertrude's turn to sit back and blink. "Closet? Why it's in the bedroom of your boarding house, of course." Then after a moment, she said, "which brings me to the second topic. Hemingway and I are trustees to the newly opened Bibliotheque Américain."

"Wait," I said. "A Bibliotheque? That's a library. Correct?"

"Yes, a library," Gertrude said, somewhat impatiently. "We opened it two years ago, back in '20, but so far, it's been a disaster. Nobody can figure out how to take books written in English out of the crates and put them up on the shelves in some sort of rhyme or reason." She shook her head. "It's really not that hard. We've gone through four directors and we're no closer to efficiently running a library than we were when we opened the front doors. That's where you two come in."

I felt myself stiffen; my eyes grew wide. Cherie grabbed my hand.

I asked, "Are you offering us a job?"

Gertrude leaned across the table and looked us in the eyes, me first then Cherie.

"More than just a job. I want you to be co-directors of the Bibliotheque Américain. We'll pay a nice salary, put you two up in the boarding house, and give you free access to the bistro across the street." She looked at Cherie. "I'm assuming by the way Thomas introduced you, one room will do. Yes?"

Cherie slowly turned and faced me. She found my eyes. "One room will do."

When my mouth, which had dropped open, began working again, I asked, "Are you saying we're staying?"

"Thomas, I know this is astonishingly quick, but I think I've already fallen in love with Paris. This is a dream come true for me. This is your dream as well. Remember last night, you said this would be your favorite time to live in. Now's our chance." She squeezed my hand and pleaded. "Let's do it. It's not like we're leaving anything behind. And unless I've been fooling myself, you and I, well, this love is real." Cherie leaned closer. "This could be the start of something great. We can do this." She paused, then, "How many times do we get an opportunity like this? If we don't stay, we'll regret the decision for the rest of our lives. Oh please. Let's stay."

Gertrude stood. "You two talk it over and let me know tonight. Alice has given me a long list of groceries to pick up. We've got a party to get ready for. Don't be late."

# Epilogue

Horace stood with his hands on his hips, staring at the piles of new books. Last week, he had purchased another private library in an estate sale. It seemed like a great idea at the time.

Meow, the cat, jumped up onto the sales counter, curled up, wrapping its tail around its body like a fur coat, and stared at Horace.

"You know, Meow, the time has come for us to hire someone to replace Thomas. Since he disappeared without a trace two weeks ago, I've had to do all this sorting and stocking. I'm not cut out for manual labor."

Horace walked to the coffee pot, refilled his mug, then plopped down onto the bottom tread of the spiral staircase.

He took a sip of coffee. "I don't understand it. It's not like him to up and vanish. He was always so, so, responsible. I think it was that blond woman's fault. Thomas would have never left on his own. I knew she was trouble from the moment I laid eyes upon her."

Meow blinked. Horace sighed.

Absently, he took the top book off the nearest stack. It was a coffee table picture book entitled *An American Photographer Living in Paris: The Complete Works of a French Surrealist, Man Ray.*

Sipping his coffee, Horace idly flipped through the

pages. Most of Man Ray's works were somewhere between odd and bizarre, but one chapter featured his portrait and photo-journalism phase. And one of those black and white pictures was a large, posed shot entitled "The Party." Horace studied the people on the page. He recognized Gertrude Stein and Hemingway and Zelda Fitzgerald. But on the left end of the line of people toasting wine glasses toward the photographer stood an unknown but hauntingly familiar couple. Abruptly, Horace put down his coffee, lumbered to his feet, and walked to his desk. There, he turned on the lamp and extracted a hand-held magnifying glass from the drawer. Slowly lowering his bulk into the wooden swivel desk chair, he studied the couple.

The woman was blond, wearing a flapper style, beaded spangly dress with matching heels. And the man wore a sport coat and cotton dress shirt, open at the neck. They were arm in arm, gazing into each other's eyes. Horace studied their faces, and after a few beats, quietly whistled.

Then he dropped the magnifier on the book and leaned back in his groaning chair. Meow had jumped down from the counter and come for a scratch behind the ears.

Horace pursed his lips. And after a moments' cogitation, he said, "Well I'll be dipped in shit. Meow my friend, Thomas has found our suitcases."

# AFTERWORD

During the COVID-19 pandemic, three writers (who also happened to be good friends) began searching for a way to beat the "stay at home" blahs. We met regularly on Zoom to discuss other writing projects, which was okay, but it was becoming apparent that we needed a new and challenging task to fire our creative juices.

Then one day, Donna suggested that we try to work cooperatively on a series of short stories. This would be done round-robin style, with the first person writing the beginning, the second the middle, and the third the ending. Each week, each of us would start a story, pass it to a second, who would pass it on to the third. At the end of the week, we would meet on Zoom and read all three completed stories. And then again the next week, and the next, and so on for five weeks. In this manner, we were always juggling three stories being written by three different writers. The pressure and incentive to keep this going resembled the game played by children known as Hot Potato.

At first, the topics were whatever struck our fancies, but eventually, we chose genres such as Historical Fiction and Science Fiction. Our goal in this exercise was to keep the voice and pacing consistent. The result of this effort is what follows. Are they all great? Nope. Not by a long shot. But some are quite good and all were challenging. If you choose to read on, be gentle. This was new territory for three people who enjoy each other's company and also enjoy writing. It got us through this damn, crazy time.

Enjoy!

Sue, Donna, and Alan

# A Boy of Good Will

By Donna, Alan, Sue

H e crept across the front lawn, one sneakered foot in front of the other. His right hand clutched a small cut-glass saltshaker, the left arm outstretched for balance. A scarlet-chested robin tugged a fat worm from the manicured yard, unaware of its prey approaching just three feet from its tail. The boy's parents supervised from the porch, covering their mouths to stifle chuckles.

"Aw, shucks! He flew away. How'd he know I was behind him? Shoot!" He put one hand on his little hip and flung some salt into the grass where the bird had been, smiling toward them.

"Ben," his father called out, "what would you do if you actually caught it?"

The child grinned, squinting into the late afternoon sun. "I'm not stopping. He could be a pet...or something."

That's one of the many fond memories they had of their son's early years. Ben always accepted a challenge, forever optimistic, never giving up. He had believed his father when he told him he could catch a bird if he sprinkled salt on its tail, and he tried to succeed that entire summer.

"Put that boy in a room full of shit and he'd be looking for the pony," his father pronounced to his wife, not for the first time. "I love that boy."

Ben's mother sighed a heartful of love herself. They had never expected such a joyful gift to come along so late in their lives. After seventeen childless years, Benjamin joined their lives. *Benjamin*, son of their lives, their daily sonshine.

They knew he was special and felt blessed. Once, when his mother saw a taller boy on his soccer team poking him and pushing him in the practice line, she sat in the car angry and distressed that Ben didn't hit him back. She chastised her son when the practice ended.

"But, Mom. What would God have thought of me if I hit him?"

Ben's turn-the-other-cheek mantra continued into high school until the inevitable happened: he became the target of the school bully. The event took place after baseball practice and all Ben's team mates had left the field. The bully, Jimmy Rainy, and his two thuggish sidekicks wandered onto the diamond where Ben was taking some solitary after-practice swings with a weighted bat. Jimmy, roughly the size of a gorilla, honed-in on Ben and wasted little time. The pushes grew into punches, and when Ben went down, turned in kicks. It was at that point, when Ben was being kicked like some whimpering stray dog, that the fight or flight syndrome activated. In a twinkling, Ben was on his feet and waded into Jimmy Rainy, throwing adrenaline-fueled punches with a madman's fury. After a frantic few minutes the two combatants separated, and glared at each other. Technically, if you were the ringside judge, the split decision would have gone to Rainy, but he was bleeding profusely from his nose and a cut over his left eye, so the fight would have been stopped by the referee. Ben was also bloodied and minus one tooth, but unlike Rainy, Ben was still game. Rainy growled, "This ain't over," then turned and walked away, flanked by his thugs. After they were out of sight, Ben collapsed in a heap and sobbed mightily.

Two days later, the baseball coach sat with Ben on the bench. Practice was over and the rest of the team was heading for the showers.

The coach was studying the starting lineup for the next day's game. Ben was packing his duffle.

"I saw Rainy in the hallway today," the coach began. "He looks like he's taken a beating."

Ben stopped arranging his gear. Tears began welling up in his eyes.

"It's been my experience," the coach continued, "that the likes of Jimmy Rainy will find another target. One that doesn't hit back."

The coach continued staring at the lineup for a few beats then asked, "How're you doing?"

Desperately holding back the tears, Ben said, "Okay I guess."

Making a correction on the sheet, the coach said, "We're alike you and me. Violence is not our thing. Maybe we think the world's greatest pacifists, Jesus, Gandhi and John Lennon, had it right, but the problem is," and at that point the coach turned and faced Ben, "The rest of the world doesn't see things the way we do. Sometimes..."

Ben kept staring at his duffle.

"That's why," the coach continued, "I became a medic in the army. It was my way of coping with violence without resorting to it. It worked for me. It was my way of fighting back."

After another few quiet beats, he stood and said, "Come on. Time for a shower."

Ben sat languidly nursing his fourth beer as Larry finished cleaning up the bar. He played with the coaster, seeing how long he could keep it spinning. It was late, and he knew that he shouldn't be walking the streets of Nagarote alone at this hour. It was one of the points his predecessor, Cameron, had made repeatedly. "You learn to love this place and its people," he had said, "but the night streets are dangerous." Still, he didn't feel like going back to his empty apartment.

He smiled as he remembered how proud and excited his parents had been when he told them he had been hired right out of college as the field director for the Two Cities Project

"I always said he'd find a way to help other people, Marnie," his father said. His mother beamed with pride while fighting to keep from tearing up. Nicaragua was a long way away, and who hadn't heard of all the gangs and drug lords in Central America? Even his old baseball coach, who had continued to be his mentor and friend beyond high school, had sent him on his new venture with cheers and good wishes.

But gangs and drug lords were not a problem here, thank heavens. The kids in the project were great; the teachers were committed; even the townspeople, generally wary of outsiders, were beginning to open up to him. No, his problem was loneliness. All the young people of his age – many of whom had been educated by the project – had left Nagarote for jobs elsewhere, in Managua or Leon or Costa Rica.

And left all alone every night, he had begun to doubt himself. Was it all worth it? Was he making a difference? Did he really need to come all the way down here to find ways to help people?

"I'm closing up, Ben," Larry called from behind the bar. "Be careful out there."

Ben heaved himself up and wandered out toward the street. "Night, Larry. See you tomorrow."

He had stayed later than usual, lost in his thoughts. The street at this hour felt different. It was quiet – too quiet - and dark. The new moon cast little light, and of course there were no streetlights. He found himself throwing his flashlight beam into doorways and down alleys and picking up his pace a bit.

Then, from out behind a milk wagon stepped a figure. Ben's whole body kicked into alert mode. He felt vulnerable – in one pocket he had his cell phone; in the other, his Swiss army knife, neither one of which was likely to be of much use against a determined aggressor.

"Jefe!" the voice called. "It's me, Mario."

He let out an audible sigh of relief, then frowned in consternation when he looked more closely at the boy, one of the best students in the project. Mario took as many courses as he could and then hung around to volunteer whenever possible. A couple of the teachers had expressed concern about occasional bruises and scrapes on his face and arms; he brushed them aside, saying that he was clumsy and had fallen, but the teachers suspected that his father was abusing him. They wanted to intercede, but Mario assured them all was fine.

As the boy came toward him, he saw that his face was battered and there was blood on his shirt.

"Good grief, Mario! What happened to you?"

"My father kicked me out of the house. Said he never wanted to see my ugly face again."

Ben hesitated. His instincts were to take the boy home and nurse him back to health, as he had done many years ago with an abandoned baby squirrel and again with a baby bird, but he heard the voices of the board members telling him not to get personally involved with the locals. It was a close-knit community with its own set of mores, and it was easy to offend. He didn't want to undo all the good will that had been built up over the 20 years that the project had been working there.

Ben looked again at the bloody face and pleading eyes of the boy before him and felt himself tearing up. "Come on home with me for the night and we'll see what we can do tomorrow."

He put his arm around the boy and started walking. Who knew where this would lead? Maybe it would turn out to be an antidote to his loneliness.

*Donna comments on A Boy of Good Will. I started this as a nod to delightful young boys who don't always "fit the mold" as aggressive kids with mischief on their minds. This first attempt as a shared story gave the boy a depth I had not considered.*

*Alan comments: I recalled a similar young boy who*

*years ago, chose the pacifist route instead of the "might makes right" direction. He in fact, was a medic in the army and served in Vietnam. I have long lost track of him but on occasion, thought about him and hope he is well.*

*Sue comments: My section of the story was based on my association with an organization called the Norwalk/Nagarote Sister City Project. During my frequent visits there, I often thought how lonely it must be for our Field Directors, idealistic young people not long out of college. It seemed a logical place for our "boy of good will" to end up.*

# COMPUTER GAMES

By Sue, Donna, Alan

"Johnny? Johnny! Time for dinner, Son." Alma called up to her son's room.

"Can't come now," a muffled voice replied. "Just got to the next level."

Fred - husband, father, and fulltime businessman - walked into the dining room.

"Fred, you have to do something about your son. He plays those stupid video games all day long. He won't listen to me. 'I already passed Winston' or 'One more level and I'll be ahead of Alfred,' he says when I ask him to stop. It's like that's the real world for him and we're just Lego figures, like he's living in a parallel universe."

Alma's hand shook slightly as she put Fred's plate in front of him – neatly partitioned, with pork chop carefully distanced from mashed potatoes, carefully distanced from green beans.

Fred took his fork and increased the separation slightly before wordlessly attacking his plate.

"And they're so violent! It's all about killing and bombing and destroying! I read someplace that spending so much time on those awful games makes people violent."

"Oh, for Christ's sake, Alma. You're blowing it all out of proportion. He's finally found something he's good at. At least he's not just playing by himself with Legos or whatever he used to do all day. He actually has friends he plays with. You babied him too much and let him just hang around the house. You never could let him go. And now you're jealous of a silly game."

"That's not fair! I am NOT jealous of his stupid games and you know it! I actually care about what happens to our son, which is more than I can say for you."

"Watch where you're going, woman. Just because I don't pamper him and give in to his every whine and whimper doesn't mean I don't care about him. I care that he becomes a man who can stand up for himself, not run home whining every time somebody says "Boo" to him. Who knows? Maybe all that make-believe aggression will put a spine in his back and some balls between his legs." Fred laughed and turned back to his plate, stabbing his pork chop for emphasis.

Alma, face red, near tears, turned from him and stomped up the stairs. "I'll make him come down," she muttered.

She opened the door to her son's room, looked over toward the computer, screamed, and fainted.

Johnny ran to the door, dragged his mother into his room, closed the door gently and slapped her face. "Mom, Mom," he hissed. "For God's sake, why didn't you knock? Wake up!" He pinched her cheeks, hard.

Alma's eyes fluttered open, then widened as she stared into her son's painted face. Before she could scream again, Johnny clamped his hand over her mouth.

"Shut the hell up. Why are you freaking out? Do you want him to come up here? Is that what you want?" He leaned into his mother's ear, whispering with desperation. "Are you trying to get me in trouble?"

Alma shook her head nervously and grabbed at the hand gripping her mouth, muffling his name.

"If you utter one sound, I swear I'll knock your head into the floor. Do you understand me?" His black eyes bore into hers, belying the huge red grin painted across his face. "I said, DO-YOU-UNDERSTAND?"

The woman lay clamped to the floor, at first shaking her head under her son's glare, then quickly nodding yes, yes, she understood. Johnny slowly lifted his hand away. "Wha--," she tried to speak quietly, but her son grabbed a handful of his mother's hair and slammed her head against the floor. "Are you stupid? I said shut the hell up. That means do not talk. Not in a whisper. Not at all." He pulled her further into the room and opened the door slightly.

"Dad?" he called out. "Mom's pissed about my messy room. Be down in a minute." The boy stood over his mother and pointed at both of his cheeks. "What's wrong, Mom, haven't you ever seen the Joker before? What's so scary about this? It's part of a game, mommy." His voice mocked a sing-song tune, and he combed his fingers through black hair, making it stand on end. "You will stay up here and clean my room, you bitch. I'm going to eat the shit you call dinner. After I wash my face, of course."

Alma pulled herself into a sitting position and propped her back against Johnny's bed. She watched her son saunter into his bathroom, shutting the door behind him. Alma stared at the bloodied dead and dying bodies on the computer screen across the room. Horrified, she couldn't look away. How is this a game, she wondered.

When Johnny emerged from the bathroom pulling a fresh white t-shirt over his head, he turned the computer off and kicked his mother's hip with heavy black boots. "Sorry, mommy," he smiled playfully. "This room is such a mess, I tripped over my dirty clothes. Do your job, lady. And then go to bed without dinner. DO-YOU-UNDERSTAND, mother dear? If you say a word to the man downstairs, who will he be upset with?"

Johnny slouched into the kitchen and slid into a chair at the table. Before looking at the food on the plate in front of him, he took out his phone and began texting to one of his pals. He never heard his father approaching from behind. He never heard the low hum of the cattle prod.

When he opened his eyes, Johnny lay in the center of the kitchen floor. His limbs were twitching, and his tongue seemed lifeless. He was unable to speak or move. His eyes spotted his dad at the kitchen table, engrossed in some sort of gadget he held in his hands.

"Welcome back, Johnny," he said without looking away from the object. "You've gone too far." He then shifted in his seat and stared down at his son. "You threatened your mother. You've gone too far." He then moved his chair from the table to where Johnny lay, sat back down, and leaned down close to his son's head. "I haven't been much of a father, or a husband I suppose, but I do have a few beliefs. At the top of my list is "thou shall not harm my wife." I know this is beyond your ability to understand, and real-life morality is foreign to you. I was willing to let you play your games, hoping you'd come around, but I was wrong. I suppose, once again I failed as a parent. But to threaten your mother with violence, well, that ain't gonna ride."

Johnny made some guttural noises, but otherwise just twitched on the floor.

"So, here's what I'm going to do," Fred said. "I'm going to speak in your language. Remember that game you used to play? Space Mercenaries? You have made it to level five as an intergalactic mercenary. This new level is far more dangerous, and you should have known that. After all, you are a skilled killer. Think of me as the emperor of a distant galaxy and your mother, well, she can be a princess. No, we aren't the loving couple we once were, but we're still allies, or co-rulers I suppose, of our galaxy. Now here you are, landing in our corner of the universe, threatening my princess. Follow so far?"

More guttural noises.

"As emperor, I am charged with defending all that is mine, and you, a ruthless killer, have been captured."

Fred got up and retrieved the cattle prod. He turned the dial up to EXTREME DANGER: WILL STOP THE HEART OF A 500 POUND BULL. The prod hummed louder.

"You have been found guilty of attempted murder." He bent over his son, and said, "As for you mister intergalactic mercenary, it's GAME OVER."

*Sue comments on Computer Games. This is NOT where I thought the story would end up, although I must admit, I didn't really know what I wanted to do with it, so I was happy to hand it off to Donna*

*Donna comments: The challenge here was to imagine where the family dynamic would take this obnoxious teen and his dysfunctional parents. Just like Sue, I was delighted to go so far, then let Alan twist the end in a surprising direction.*

*Alan comments: Wouldn't it be wonderful if bad guys really could be handled this way!*

# Dame Lizzy Advises

## By Alan, Sue, Donna

"Five thousand dollars."

The frumpy, gray-haired woman with cat-eye floral-frame thick glasses looked up at me from where she sat in her folding chair behind the card table.

"I'm sorry sir, but the price is firm. Twenty thousand dollars for the entire library."

I removed my wallet and extracted a credit card. "Look, this is the final day of the estate sale. If those books were going to sell, they would have gone over the weekend. In four hours, the sale is over, and the entire collection will be hauled off to some auction with the rest of the unsold items." Then for added effect, I leaned down and lowered my voice. "You make twenty-five percent of the take. If those books are still here at five tonight, you'll make twenty five percent of nothing." I held out my VISA. "Twenty five percent of five grand is a whole lot better. Don't you think?"

The next morning, it took three hours to unload all the books from my rusting Land Rover and carry them into my library in the barn. It wouldn't have taken so long but Dame Lizzy insisted upon sprawling in the patch of sunlight just inside the door. I had to repeatedly step over and around her.

"You could move, you know," I said, more than once. She fixed me with her huge brown watery eyes and once, even thumped her tail a few times. Dame Lizzy was a dog of unknown lineage, perhaps a cross between a Labrador Retriever and an elephant. She was ten which in dog years, made us the same age - seventy.

I meticulously removed each Agatha Christie hardcover – some first editions! - and arranged them by publication date on the shelves of honor alongside my leather over-stuffed chair. I'd unload the balance of the collection on eBay and maybe break even. No matter. It was the Christies I wanted. A dream come true.

Upon sliding *Elephants Can Remember* – the final Poirot novel – into place, I stood back to admire my new collection.

"Lizzy, my girl, guess what I'll be reading when the snow flies."

Dame Lizzy thumped her tail once.

I randomly picked one of her earlier books, *The Mysterious Affair at Styles,* and sat upon the leather ottoman to give it a look. As I opened the near-mint condition volume, two pieces of paper fell out from the dust cover and fluttered to the floor. I retrieved them both. The first was an official looking Wells Fargo bank receipt for a safety deposit box, and the second was a handwritten note with the following:

*row 3, box j47*
*279-35-91apw397 pin 204*

I stared at the two pieces of paper while myriad possibilities swirled through my mind.

"Holy shit, old girl," I said. "If this means what I think it does, we're in for a wild ride."

Lizzy looked up at me archly. She didn't approve of profanity but was nonetheless interested, so she heaved herself up, wandered over to me, and nuzzled my leg for attention. I reached down distractedly, my mind rehearsing various scenarios, and patted her head. Lizzie nuzzled again – she didn't do "distractedly"; she wanted my full attention.

"What do you think could be in the box?" I asked her, this time looking right into those great big brown eyes. "And why would she have kept the papers here, in this book? Was she hiding them from someone? Or was she just some absent-minded old lady who put things somewhere and forgot about them?"

Lizzie greeted my last hypothesis with a snort. She expected more of me. As you have undoubtedly surmised, I am an inveterate mystery reader. What I love about the genre is that I can match my wits against the sleuth, whether it be Sherlock or Poirot or Jack Reacher. I always run my suspicions past Lizzie, of course, so I consider her my partner in crime, so to speak.

"Well, I guess the best way to find out is to go to the bank and check it out." I started to collect myself and get moving, but then thought, "Uh oh! What if I need some kind of ID? Hmm."

I hadn't spent all that time reading mysteries for nothing. Elizabeth Jordan had identified all her books by writing her name clearly on the flyleaf of each. I practiced until I felt sure of myself, went to my computer and began writing.

"Here it is, Lizzie, worthy of Hercule himself," I said as I presented a piece of paper and read its contents to her.

*I, Elizabeth Jordan, give my nephew, Bartholomew Higgins, access to my Wells Fargo safe deposit box.*

*Signed, Elizabeth Jordan*

Lizzie sniffed, lifted her head high, and turned to walk toward her favorite spot in front of the door, displaying in full her regal backside. She did not approve of chicanery of any sort; it only led to more trouble.

My one-hour drive into town the next day led to random possibilities, all with negative conclusions. Lizzie offered no support and insisted on staring out the passenger-side window, clearly disapproving of my deceitful plan. "Come on, girl. Be a good sport. What could go wrong?"

The dog offered a condescending glance my way, which said a lot, considering our history and the dozens of times my curiosity had led to, well, unhealthy results.

As luck would have it, the parking spot in front of Wells Fargo Bank perfectly accommodated my Land Rover. I reached across Lizzie to roll her window up just far enough to prevent an escape. She sighed and curled up on the seat.

"Don't give up on me, girl. I have a good feeling about this. If I'm lucky enough to hit the jackpot, we can get a new car, with air conditioning!"

It took a moment for my eyes to adjust to the typically shaded bank's interior. "Good morning, ma'am. I need to get some things out of my safe deposit box," I said calmly, pulling the receipt from my wallet.

"I need to see some identification, sir."

"Of course, of course. Here you go." I handed over my driver's license, feigning no discomfort. I had decided to hold off showing the note from my "Aunt" Elizabeth unless asked for more validation.

"Come with me, sir."

I glanced out the front window to give Lizzie a thumb's up, but she continued to show no interest in my deceit. The bank teller's equal disinterest relieved me, but I was disappointed that I didn't get to flaunt the forged permission slip.

My hands shook as I held the key, searching for row 3, box j47. When I slid the box out of its cubby hole, my heart danced. It felt so light, I knew it couldn't hold anything heavy, like a book or even gold jewelry. Money was my objective, and I held my breath as I keyed in the pin number.

"What the hell? How in the world...?" I folded the single piece of paper and placed it back in the envelope. My mission complete, I returned the key to the teller and sauntered back to my rusty old car.

"Well, Lizzie, you were wrong, old girl. No harm, no foul. It's the title to a car, so there."

I had no idea how the title ended up in my nonexistent aunt's safety deposit box, but I was determined to get to the bottom of the mystery. At least now, if I ever did decide to sell my Land Rover, I finally had the legal paperwork to prove it belonged to me.

*Alan comments on Dame Lizzy Advises. I had to come up with something, so I wrote this story based upon my love of Agatha Christie novels. And incidentally, I'd gladly pay five-thousand dollars for a collection of Agatha's books! This tale did not go where I thought it might. One of the greatest aspects of this entire exercise was to see where the story goes. Great fun.*

*Sue comments: I loved the character of Dame Lizzy and had fun developing her.*

*Donna comments: At first, I had no idea where to take the humor or the dog, as neither is my strong suit. The surprising part was that once my "voice" picked up where Alan began and Sue continued, it was fun to venture outside of my comfort zone.*

# Dame Lizzy Negotiates

By Alan, Donna, Sue

Feet up on my ottoman, I nestled into my over-stuffed leather chair. Agatha Christie's <u>Murder at End House</u> lay on my lap. Three fingers of bourbon awaited my attention within arm's reach on the end table. The final task in this joyous ritual was to pack my pipe. This was heaven.

Lizzie lay sprawled on the oak floor, absorbing the heat radiating from the wood stove in the corner. I had kindled a small fire to chase the evening chill. At 7,000 feet, warm summer nights are nonexistent.

I struck a match and was about to fire up the tobacco when I noticed Lizzie had gotten to her feet and was now staring at the mirror which hung on the far wall.

"Oh shit," I said. "Not again."

Retrieving the mirror, I returned to my chair and propped it up upon my lap. As expected, immediately behind my reflection stood a man. He had a high forehead, sandy hair combed straight back, and sported a neatly trimmed moustache. He wore his starched, high-collar white shirt, and a gold chain connected the pockets of his tweed vest. His nervous blue eyes darted side to side.

"Well, if it isn't Horatio McCallister," I said. "To what do I owe the pleasure?"

"So sorry to intrude and of course, if it wasn't a matter of utmost importance..."

"Save the speech, Horatio," I exclaimed. "I thought we had agreed to co-exist without intruding upon each other?"

"So right, so right, and I offer nothing but apologies but..."

"Weren't you just here a month ago with the crisis du jour?"

Horatio stiffened. "Are you referring to those gothic beasts which invaded my domicile?"

"We call those bats. They're harmless, especially to the likes of you. And by previous agreement, you live in the attic. So do they."

"Well..."

"And by the way, what was the point of your little prank with the title to my car in the safety deposit box?"

Horatio smiled weakly and twisted his hands together. "That actually brings me to the point of my visit."

"I wasn't very happy about that wild goose chase. Keep in mind, I've got a friend who deals in commercial real estate and has offered a huge pile of cash for this very house we share. He's a phone call away and presto, this place we call home would turn into a Home Depot, complete with expansive paved parking lot and maybe even a Starbucks. I could pick up a place with a mountain view and live happily ever after. You on the other hand, would have to go back to haunting the local Baptist Church."

Horatio folded his arms and raised his chin. "Empty threats don't become you Mr. Bartholomew Higgins."

I exhaled. "Yeah, you're right. But let's get back to the point of this meeting. What's up this time?"

Horatio went back to wringing his hands. "You may not know this, but I have a lady friend."

I nearly dropped the mirror. "You what? No kidding! A girlfriend? When..."

"Lady who is a friend. Not *girlfriend*. Well, not yet anyways."

"So, tell me. When did this happen?"

"We met at Lincoln's funeral."

"Lincoln as in *Abraham* Lincoln, the 16th president?"

"The same."

"That was over 150 years ago!"

Ignoring my pronouncement, he leaned closer. "And she's lovely. I'm sure you'll agree. Her name is Clara and she'll be no trouble, I guarantee."

My mouth fell open. When my temporary dumbness passed, I said, "Hold on there, bucko. What's this all about?"

"Her house is being torn down to make way for absolutely tasteless condominiums and she will be put out on the street. So, I thought, perhaps, if you agree, which I know you will because you have such a kind and generous disposition, she could come here and live with us." He blinked hopefully.

"And just out of curiosity, what does that have to do with your little joke and the safety deposit box?"

"Well, you see. I needed to get you out of the house so I could show Clara around..."

"So, she's been here already?"

"And she just *loves* what you've done to the place. She did say those brown curtains will have to go and there'll be no more smoking your pipe indoors and she really likes your bedroom but..."

"WHAT? My bedroom?"

"Oh, she simply adores the view from your bay window."

I looked at Lizzy who was staring at me with those big doleful eyes.

"Did you know anything about this?"

Lizzy pasted her ears back.

I took a few steadying breaths. "Let's say, hypothetically of course, that I agree to let Clair..."

"Clara."

"Fine. Clara. Let's say I agree to let her move in temporarily, just until she can find a place of her own. Why can't she move in with you in the attic?"

Horatio stiffened. "Surely, you are not suggesting we live together!"

"Why not? The attic is enormous."

"Our relationship has not progressed anywhere near that sort of arrangement. I don't know what you think of me but surely..."

"IT'S BEEN 155 YEARS!"

We stared at each other in the mirror, then I shook my head slowly. "I need some time to think about this."

Horatio once again began wringing his hands.

"Time?"

"Yeah. I don't know if this will work..."

"But Clara will be here in five minutes."

I returned the mirror to the wall, grabbed my bourbon and stared at the dog. Dame Lizzy gazed at me with that familiar look of innocence, which inevitably meant she was not.

"What are you looking at? Did you know anything about this? How am I going to get out of this one?"

Lizzy heaved herself up from a comfortable sprawl,

circled herself twice and rested right back in front of the wood stove. She steadied her doleful brown eyes and waited for me to take a swig and sit back down.

"All I want to do is savor the great steal I made in purchasing this wonderful Christie collection and read my favorite book. Now that old coot Horatio has to come out and haunt me with his shenanigans. Again."

I sat back down, repropped my feet on the ottoman, and grabbed my pipe. "Can't I have a moment's peace? Five minutes, my foot! He'll appear when I say he can appear, and I'm not looking in that mirror again tonight. The nerve of that S-O-B, hiding that note and sending me out on a wild goose chase. For what? For nothing, that's what."

Lizzy lifted her head ever so slightly, a muffled sigh coming from her closed mouth.

"Well, nothing other than returning my car title, which the old goat probably swiped from my file in the attic in the first place."

Lizzy thumped her tail and closed her eyes.

Lighting my pipe, I settled back in to remember the intricate twists and turns Christie wove around Hercule Poirot's clever detective work. One of the greatest clues lay in the fact that the characters' names hid the killer from most readers until the end. I had figured it out early on, of course, but only because I was a student of Agatha Christie's brilliant genre.

"Just remember, Dame Lizzy, names are important. A great author doesn't just throw out the name of a character from the air. A great author *designs* characters' names deliberately, with a purpose."

Now Lizzy understood that I was on to something, so she sat up on her haunches and stared me down.

"What now? I don't care about Horatio's threat to bring some broad into my humble abode. Five minutes, five hours, five days. It's my house. I decide when guests arrive and where they stay, apparitions or not!"

The great dog lumbered over to my resting legs and nuzzled them, then pushed them off of the ottoman, propping her muzzle where my feet had been.

"Do you know something about this? Is it the clue about names? Is that what you're reacting to, old girl?"

Her wholesome bark belied her old age, energized that I was closing in on the problem. She continued to stare.

I rested the ivory-bowled pipe in its tray, finished off my bourbon, and held up the book, finger holding its place. "Is that it? Does a name ring a bell for you? What name?"

Since both feet were already on the floor, I stood and studied my prized collection of first-edition books. "A steal, indeed. She did acquiesce to my demands awfully quickly, didn't she? Let me see." I perused my expensive collection, took a breath and smacked my forehead.

"Let's go Lizzy. That old broad swindled me and I'm getting my money back."

I made the mistake of looking in the mirror as I grabbed my keys from the chairside table. Mesmerized, I watched Horatio appear with a big smile on his face. "What the hell are you looking at? And where's your girlfriend? What's her name, Clair--?"

Horatio said nothing but shook his head at me with a clear sense of pity.

Lizzy barked, with more energy this time, then she jumped up onto her master's chest and knocked the book out of my hands.

"This is a first edition, you old canine. Take care!"

Lizzy was clearly insulted and left a gaseous exhaust as she turned from me and headed toward the door.

"Names. What's in a name? A title? Look at these. *Murder on the Orient Distress*, *And Then There Were Some*, *Partners in Time*, and for Pete's sake, *Peril at End House*??? It's 'murder', and that old coot better hope I don't get my hands on her before the police arrive." I took one last look in the mirror.

"Clara is my friend's name. That was the hint. Your dog caught on, even if you didn't," Horatio taunted good-naturedly. "And you think you're such a student of Agatha Christie."

The rusty old Land Rover started up after only three attempts, and Lizzy posted her head out of the passenger window, satisfied.

"O.K., O.K., so you were on to something after all. It's my influence over you that has made you so smart. Agatha Christie's mother's name was Clara. I should have caught the clue."

I pushed the old Land Rover aggressively. The closer I came to the address on the business card I held tightly in my hand, the more agitated I became.

"Five thousand dollars," I mumbled. "I can't believe I paid five thousand dollars for a counterfeit set of Christies. Wait till I get that woman." My jaw tightened, and I clenched and unclenched my fists. I looked over at Dame Lizzie who shook her head disgustedly. "It wasn't my fault. I mean really. Somebody went to a hell of a lot of trouble to make those books look real – tattered leather cover, slightly blurred titles so you wouldn't notice the changes, brittle pages.

Lizzie raised her eyebrow – sort of – and gave me her "What- are- you- going- to- do -about- it" look.

"You don't have to be so judgmental. I suppose I should just go to the police, but I want to confront the old bat. Maybe I'll just play dumb and act as if I want her to help me buy some more books. Get the goods on her. Poirot would do something like that."

I approached the address cautiously. I had driven through town to a more sparsely settled area. Large trees lined the street, and the houses, old and in varying stages of disrepair, were spaced well apart.

"Number 1752 should be right ahead, old girl. There it is, I think. I can barely see the house for the hedges and shrubs. I think I'd better park here and go the rest of the way on foot."

I sighed, got out of the car, and had started to walk toward the house before Lizzie let out a sharp yap that let me know she was not at all in agreement with my actions.

"I think it will be better if I confront her alone, old girl." I looked at her through the window, thinking foolishly that she would of course see how reasonable I was being. My mistake was in looking at her. "Oh, okay. Come on." I opened the door and Lizzie jumped out, but she held back.

"What's the matter? You don't think we should go right in?" Lizzie sat down.

"The place does look a bit suspicious – all those bushes could be hiding something. Maybe we should just check out the place before we go in."

Lizzie gave me the "Duh!" look, got up, and started to snake through the bushes to the back of the house. While Lizzie is indeed big, she is still a dog and can go places that humans have difficulty following. I struggled to keep up with her, branches slapping me, briars snagging me. When she emerged a few minutes later, she sat down and panted expectantly. In front of us, half hidden by more shrubs, was a building, considerably larger than your typical back yard shed.

"Will you look at that?" I said, pulling twigs out of my hair and briars off my sleeve. "I say we creep over and have a look . . ." Lizzie, unable to wait for me to finish, had already assumed the doggie version of the marine crawl and was heading toward the building. I ducked down and tiptoed behind her.

The lone window was set up so high that I had to stand on tiptoes to see in. It was dark inside but I was able to make out the contents of the building.

"Books, Lizzie! Rows and rows of books. I was right! We've stumbled onto a big counterfeiting business." In my excitement, I failed to notice Lizzie's look that said "Stumbled? I don't think so."

"Come on! We're getting in there somehow." I walked around to the door and checked the lock. "This doesn't look very complicated." I took out a credit card and slid it around between the door and the jamb.

At first, I was afraid it wasn't going to work, and I don't have a large repertoire of lock-picking tricks, but then the lock released and we were in. I flicked on the flashlight on my keyring – a staple for every sleuth – and gasped at what I saw – every shelf filled with books like the set I had bought for five thousand dollars. Only they weren't just Agatha Christies. The titles were faded and hard to read. I pulled out one and looked closely at it – David Cooperfield, and another, Oliver Tryst. There was a whole set of Shakersbeer – Hairy IVy, and Harlet, and Ofello.

ALAN MULAK, DONNA SMITH, SUE PASCUCCI

While I was lost in checking out the vast array of cleverly altered titles, Lizzie was doing her own sleuthing. She caught my attention when she knocked over a small table in the corner.

"Good grief, girl! I can't take you any place!" As I walked over to straighten up the mess she had made, I reached down and picked up a notebook. "What the h. . .?" I opened it to the first page, on which was written:

*CLARA Publishing Company*
   *Classics*
   *Lifted*
   *And*
   *Reconfigured*
   *Artistically*

*For a nominal price you can have an authentic-looking set of classics to grace your bookshelf. Nobody ever reads them anyway.*

A casual flip through the pages revealed that I was holding in my hand the accounts of CLARA Co. – evidence enough to put them in jail for a long time.

I slipped the book inside my jacket and said, "Come on, old girl. We need to get out of here before someone discovers us. We'll decide our next steps once we're in the clear."

All the way back home, I put forth various options, but Lizzie did not respond positively to any of them. As the old Land Rover pulled into the driveway, I remembered what was waiting for me as soon as I got through the door, and my elation fizzled like a leaky balloon.

And indeed, before I even reached my favorite leather chair, Horatio appeared with Clara in tow. I covered my face with my hands, shook my head and said, "No, no, no. I can't deal with this now."

"Really, Bartholomew, you can forego the histrionics. We have very good news. Clara has decided that as long as you give her a free hand decorating the attic, she would be willing to live up there with me – once we were married, of course. So, if you will see to that small detail, we will be very happy to leave you undisturbed – relatively, of course."

I had no idea how you would get two ghosts married, but that was a problem for another day. Right now, I dismissed the ghosts, poured myself a bourbon, and lit my pipe. I picked up the book, curious to see if they had made any alterations in the story that only an inveterate Christie reader could catch. Actually, I had to admit that the whole thing was quite ingenious. Still, I needed to figure out my next steps in this case.

Lizzie had settled in her favorite spot and was looking at me for some final words.

I held up my glass and said, "Good job, old girl. We'll get those counterfeiters yet, but tomorrow is another day."

*Alan's comments: This story, the next in the Dame Lizzy adventures, was inspired by my friend and great writer, Marcy Abbott. She had written a ghost tale and the spirit could only be seen in a mirror, so I borrowed the really unique concept and created Horatio McCallister. And oh, by the way, once again the tale veered off my intended course. Thank you, Marcy. Good work Donna and Sue.*

*Donna's comments: This time I embraced Lizzy's character and really had fun throwing a wrench in the direction Alan had begun. Then I just threw it to Sue to finish!*

*Sue's comments: I had no idea what to do with this one, so I just started writing and let my pen solve the mystery.*

# DIRTY LAUNDRY

### By Sue, Alan, Donna

Primrose McQuade had a secret. In fact, there were many parts of her past life best kept under wraps.

"Never air your dirty laundry in public," her Granny had said.

Given the truth of that old adage, she had a whole basket of soiled clothes tucked away in her metaphoric cellar.

"Good night, Pumpkin," Primrose whispered as she bent down to kiss her four-year-old daughter. "Sleep tight, and don't let the bedbugs bite."

"Mommy, why do you always say that? It kinda scares me." Mia looked up at her with wide eyes.

"Really? It's just some silly old thing my Granny used to say whenever she came in to kiss me good night – even when I was way too old to need someone to tuck me in."

"It makes me think of giant bugs with pointy teeth hiding under the covers, waiting to get me as soon as you turn out the light." Mia pulled the blanket up to her chin and wriggled down into the bed.

"Good heavens, Pumpkin, why didn't you tell me

that before? I would never have kept on saying that if I had known it frightened you. "

"Why did your Granny say such scary things to you? Was she mean?"

"Oh no, baby. My Granny was a very special person. And she had a saying for every occasion. If I told her that I didn't like someone because they looked weird, she'd say "Don't judge a book by its cover." And if I was hesitant about trying something new, she'd say "Nothing ventured, nothing gained." And if I complained that we never had enough money to buy things I wanted, she'd say, "The best things in life are free.""

Mia looked puzzled. "That's silly, Mommy. Just like 'Don't let the bed bugs bite.'" She screwed up her face the way she always did when she was thinking hard. "How come I don't have a Granny like you did."

"Oh, Baby. That's a story for another day. Now, you need to close your eyes and go to sleep."

Primrose sat for a few minutes until Mia relinquished her fight to stay awake. Then she leaned over, kissed her softly, and went downstairs. Her husband wasn't home – working late again – so she poured herself another glass of wine and went outside to sit on the patio and watch the summer night slowly unfold.

Mia's questions had taken her to a place in her memory file she struggled to keep closed off. Granny emerged clothed in her pink gingham dress and sensible shoes. She was old even for a granny. Primrose's mom, Alyson, had been a late-in-life gift to Granny, whose husband departed just before her birth. Granny did her best trying to raise Alyson while working part-time at Mr. Tiburzi's Grocery Store, but somehow, it wasn't enough, and Alyson had run off following the Grateful Dead, rejecting her old-fashioned mother and slipping cheerfully into the world of casual drugs, sex, and folk rock. Primrose was the result of a one-night stand somewhere on the back streets of San Francisco, and Granny had been mother and father to her.

It wasn't her childhood she sought to erase. Primrose had connected with Granny on a special plane. Sure, her classmates and their parents looked at her pityingly when she showed up for back-to-school night or the Christmas concert, but Primrose pushed them aside to nestle into Granny's old-timey cocoon. No, it was what had happened later, when she was in her teens, that was snared in the cobwebs of her memory.

The jocks and cheerleaders had no time for the likes of Primrose and her constant companions, Mel and Gina. In fact, to the "in-crowd," they were, like so many others, invisible.

The hang-out for the popular people was the Jameson House – a spooky, abandoned, former estate that had been going back to nature for about fifty years. Little kids were terrified of it and only approached on a dare. But at this time, it had become the Saturday night haunt for all those on the inside. It was home for the usual teen-age drinking and sexual adventures. And of late, pot smoking had also been added to the pleasurable diversions.

It was an all too familiar tale: for many reasons, Primrose and Mel and Gina hated the prima donnas. They dreamed of schemes to get them into trouble and knock them off their pedestal. And then one day, their dreams became reality and they put into action a plan that would not only tarnish all the golden people but perhaps destroy their full boat scholarships at the same time.

The plan was simple. The next Saturday, at about ten pm, Gina would drop a dime and call the police, complaining of a disturbance at the Jameson House. At the same time Primrose and Mel would set fire to the wrap around porch out back. If all went according to plan, the cops would arrive about the same time the cool kids would be fleeing the Jameson House, right into the waiting arms of the local officers.

The plan worked perfectly. Or did it.

Right at 10 PM, Mel and Primrose torched the back porch. But then the wind kicked up and fanned the flames of the old wooden structure like a blacksmith's forge. In a terrifyingly short period of time, the entire structure was engulfed.

Next, the cool kids came fleeing from the burning structure just as planned – when the police were pulling up. So far, so good. They were booked and charged with a variety of crimes. That's the good news.

The bad news, really bad in fact, is there were two from the gang unaccounted for. Unbeknownst to the others, they had slipped upstairs for some privacy. Their remains were found a few days later when the fire marshal was sifting through the charred and collapsed Jameson House.

The crimes against the in-crowd were increased to negligent homicide and the cool kids were destroyed for life.

Mel died in Vietnam two years later. Gina OD'd the same year.

Then, when Granny slipped into a coma on her

death bed, Primrose fessed up and confessed her horrific crime to the most important person in her life. It was too late. There was no relief. The vivid memory of that night remained fixed in the darkest corner of Primrose's mind.

Primrose had lived with her Granny's last words for thirteen years, tucked away with the rest of her dirty laundry, but always there, always with a haunting question. What did she mean by that familiar piece of wisdom? Haunted by the dying words, Primrose persevered to make the best of the rest of her life.

And now Mia, at seventeen, mirrored a perfect reflection of everything Primrose had envied years ago. Her long blonde hair and slender, tanned body bore such confidence that her mother sometimes just stood in awe of the girl. She was forever grateful that Granny had taken her in, sheltered from the embarrassment her own mother would have brought, and encouraged her to get her degree.

"You don't need to feel obliged to apply to my alma mater, Mia. Your grades and all the leadership positions you've held will get you in anywhere. Full academic scholarship. Undisputed."

"I know, Mom. My counselor feels sure of that, too. It's just that all other juniors on the cheering squad are applying to schools with legacy status, and I want to do the same. Campus sororities look at that kind of thing. It's important."

Primrose rolled her eyes, wondering where her daughter got such high and mighty ideas. Her own career path in medical research had taken off splendidly and her six-figure income enabled the three of them to escape "the projects." Her Granny lived only long enough to see them settle in the suburbs and Mia accepted into a prestigious private day school. Then she had her stroke.

"Mia," Primrose warned the lucky girl, "remember that following along with the crowd is not always best. Think for yourself and don't try to be a prima donna."

Mia laughed heartily. "I love being a prima donna. Losers are lame. My friends and I are the people everybody envies. We are the winners, Mom. Who wouldn't want to follow us and be like us?" She tossed another blouse on the floor. "I have nothing to wear tonight. Can't I please go to the mall for just one hour? I promise I'll be back to have dinner with you before I go out. Pretty, pretty please, Mommy."

She could never resist those joyful blue eyes, though she knew she should put her foot down and hold to her earlier claims that money didn't grow on trees, a favorite of her Granny's sayings. "Oh, Pumpkin, you are such a beggar. Do not spend one cent more than thirty dollars and be back here before six o'clock. I mean it. And, young lady, pick up these clothes you have discarded as "nothing" and hang them back up before you go." She sat on the bed as if to supervise the clean-up.

"Mommy, stop with the Pumpkin thing, will you? It's SOOO embarrassing. If you want me home by six, I don't have time to hang these rags back up." Mia fixed a steely gaze on her mother, stooping to make direct eye contact. "I'll do it. Just leave, please."

As soon as Primrose left the room, Mia closed the door behind her, grabbed up the discarded outfits and crammed them into her dirty laundry basket. "There.

Perfect, just like me." She gave her hair one last fluff, put on some lipstick, and stuck her phone in her faded jeans pocket.

When Mia emerged at the bottom of the stairs, she yelled toward her mother's office. "I'm spending more than thirty dollars, just so you know. I have to get, and probably some earrings to go with whatever I have to buy *in a hurry*, so we can have a Mommy-daughter dinner. It better be good."

Primrose came into the hallway with a handful of photographs. "I just ran across these in a box. This one is so cute of you and Linda. I think you two were just starting second grade. Where does she plan to go to college?"

"Are you serious, now? Here I am being pressured to speed shop as 'time waits for no man,' as your famous Granny used to say, and you're asking me about Loony Lindy? Linda the Lard-o? Lunatic Linda with the mousey hair and wire-rimmed glasses? That girl? Really?"

"You were such good friends all through grade school. What happened?"

"What happened, Mommy, is I got cool and she didn't. She and her goofy friends follow us around with threatening stares. Matter of fact, she had the audacity to come up to my locker yesterday and ask me if I was going to Jackson Height's party! Duh!! Now, may I please be excused? You better make that dinner plan for six thirty. All this chatter is killing me!"

Primrose returned to her office and stared at the black and white photo before returning it to the box and shoving it back in the bottom drawer of her desk. She felt haunted by Mia's attitude and her sweet Granny's dying words. There was no point in trying to fix a dinner her perfect child would eat, so she put her head back and closed her eyes. She'd just order pizza.

The phone rang, startling Primrose to look at her watch. Ten thirty. The phone rang again. On the third ring, she picked up and said, "I know."

"Ms. McQuade? This is Deputy Lancaster with the sheriff's department. "I'm afraid there's been an accident."

"I know. My Granny warned me. 'What goes around, comes around.' I'm sorry."

"Ma'am?"

*Sue's Comments: This was another one I didn't see coming. Part of the fun of our experiment was sharing the completed stories and seeing where our darlings had traveled once we turned them loose.*

*Alan's Comments: This was a stretch for me. More than once in my life, I had imagined such a hairbrained scheme but fortunately, never follow-up on my dream. The most I ever did was toss a roll of toilet paper or two over their house. Writing the section as I did was the "unintended consequence" we always speak about. What a nightmare!*

*Donna's Comments: We seemed to be getting more comfortable with each other's pacing and I let this one go to its inevitable conclusion.*

# NEIGHBORHOOD CODES

### By Donna, Sue, Alan

Gloria and Mark had never really lived in a neighborhood. She had grown up in city apartments with her parents and younger sister and he was raised on a ranch with his parents and three older brothers. They met on a blind date their junior year in college and had never been apart since. Love at first sight took them from dormitory life to a small apartment, then on to resident housing while Mark finished graduate school and medical internships.

Their mutual decision to make city life a permanent base satisfied both of their careers, with Mark accepting residency at the University's state-of-the-art oncology department and Gloria soon earning the position as editor of the city's weekly event publication.

Except for the fact that they were never able to have children, their lives spun along perfectly. Once they realized how free their childless status left them, they embraced every opportunity to travel and live well.

"We have arrived, literally and figuratively," Mark quipped, escorting his wife out of their private penthouse elevator. "Look at that view!"

Gloria stepped out of her Borgezie Stilettos and

glided across the expansive foyer. "We have earned this view and everything within these walls, Dr. Ferguson. Should I even call them walls? More glass than wall. Can you imagine the Rogers or the Sampsons living here, with all their kids threatening to break everything in sight?"

They laughed and toasted each other in celebration of a life well lived. "Here's to the Ferguson abode, home of the rich and famous!"

Years passed. They traveled and entertained, ate well and collected priceless art objects. They loved their work and their things and their status. But inevitably, things had to end, as mandatory retirements forced them both to consider an "afterlife." That's what Mark called it on their way to dine with John Skipwith, longtime friend and financial advisor.

"Just like everything else in your lives, your portfolio is perfect." He moved his dessert plate to make room for the file on their private dining table. "As we've discussed before, the time is right to move out of the city and embrace all that a slower, more lucrative lifestyle can offer. That place down South is full of professional retirees just like the two of you, and your money will last you for years, even if you continue to spend lavishly." He laughed then, certain they had considered the option of wasting money if they stayed up North.

In less than six months, Dr. and Mrs. Ferguson had settled into their large manor home down South and lived, for the very first time in their lives, right in the middle of an affluent retirement community, with homes and yards within eyesight of their own. At first the lifestyle fit them well, as they decorated their home to look much like the penthouse they had left behind. Gloria and Mark were busy settling in to the next stage of their perfect life.

When the doorbell rang incessantly that first Monday morning, they expected to greet the delivery truck with some on-line items they had ordered. The woman dressed in bright green spandex surprised them.

"Well, hello. I tried to wait until you had relaxed and settled in before I came over to introduce myself, but I just couldn't wait another day. I'm your left-side neighbor Candace. Can I come in? I just want to see what you've done with the place." She squeaked in on white tennis shoes and sat down on the sofa in front of the fireplace. "Looks nice, considering. I'm sure you can get it more homey after you've been here a while. Make yourself more comfortable too."

Gloria looked at Mark, clearly puzzled. "We are comfortable."

"Well, I mean, you don't have to wear makeup all the time. For Pete's sake, it's nine thirty in the morning. I was actually hoping to see you in your pj's. We're neighbors, you know."

"I have a ten o'clock tee time," Mark glared. "I'm sure Gloria will show you around." He left the house, flashing Gloria a wide-eyed question mark.

"Uh, I've been up since six-thirty, so I've dressed for the day."

"Oh, you're one of those la-te-da ladies, huh?" Candace changed her tone with Mark out of the house.

"You've got a lot to learn. For one thing, I noticed on the neighborhood website that you do not have anyone listed as a next of kin, for emergencies, you know."

Stunned, Gloria explained that their lawyer had all of their personal information.

"Well, what if your house catches on fire and you're not home? At least give me your garage code number so I can come in and put the fire out, or see if you're both dying of asphyxiation. What's your garage code number? We all know each other's in this cul-de-sac. C'mon, give it up, Gloria."

She had been afraid to tell Mark about the personal inquisition Candace had put her through. Embarrassed, really. The final straw occurred the next week, shortly after Gloria had returned from a nighttime stroll. Mark had flown to St. Louis earlier for a Doctors without Borders seminar, and she had waited to have dinner after her walk. She stood in the kitchen deciding to fix an omelet and bacon when she heard her garage roll up. Then her phone rang.

"It's Candace. I'm in your garage in case you wondered. The wind is starting to kick up and I thought you should bring in your flag. I did it for you, so thank me very much. Are you alone?"

Gloria had been looking forward to a nice quiet evening, reading her current novel while she ate, then watching *Sense and Sensibility*, which Mark would agree, reluctantly, to watch with her, but it was so much better without his occasional comments.

"Hi Candace. Thanks for bringing it in." She let several seconds lapse, hoping that by some miracle, Candace would take the hint and leave.

"I'm free this evening, and I notice your hubby's car is gone, so we can have our own little hen party." Apparently, Candace did not take the hint.

"Um... sure." Gloria went to the door to let her in, but found that she was several steps ahead of her.

She held up a bottle of merlot and said, "I brought my own wine. We do that around here. That way nobody has to have their stash depleted. I'll just get a glass and pour it myself."

Gloria tried to keep her jaw from dropping to the floor as she watched Candace rifling through her cabinets to find the wine glasses.

"Wow! You've got some pretty fancy dishes and glassware. You'll find that we don't go much for china and crystal around here. We're definitely into 'casual.'"

"Look, Candace, why don't you go on into the living room and have a seat. I'll fix up a little snack for us."

As soon as she left, Gloria put away her plans for dinner, threw some crackers and cheese on a plate and went on into the living room. She gasped in horror as she saw Candace handling her priceless Ming vase as if it were a piece of Corning Ware.

"You have lots of interesting stuff here," she said, moving on to a French tapestry. "Looks like you travel a lot."

"Well, yes. We enjoy visiting other countries, meeting different people and learning about their history and culture."

"How many countries have you done?" Candace asked, fingering a carved statue from Mali.

"Excuse me? What do you mean by 'done'?"

"You know, how many countries have you been to? We've done 28. The Magnanos have done 34, but we'll catch up a bit this September. We're taking a cruise to the Scandinavian countries. It's our ninth cruise. How many have you been on?"

"Actually, we've never taken a cruise."

"Really? Oh, my dear, you *must* take one. Maybe you could join us. They might still have room. Once you've taken one, you will never travel any other way. For one thing, you don't have to go to a new hotel every night – and some of the places we've stopped, like Nicaragua or Brazil, you really wouldn't want to trust those hotels. The food is great, and there's nightly entertainment. Plus, it's safe. You never know about those foreigners."

Candace was still talking, but Gloria could no longer hear her. She had sunk into a quiet underwater world, where she could see a blurry face burbling and making gestures, but since she no longer had a need to connect, she floated peacefully, like a jellyfish.

At ten that evening, Gloria was sitting in her favorite chair, nursing her third – or maybe it was her fourth, she couldn't be sure – glass of wine, when Mark called to check in from St. Louis.

"Hey, Babe!" he chirped, filled with the enthusiasm of a productive conference. "How's it going?"

"Please remind me. Whose stupid-ass idea was it to spend our final years and sail off into the sunset in this intellectual and cultural desert? And yes, I know I mixed my metaphors."

"Candace, again, huh? I'm so sorry."

"Do you have any idea how many countries we've *done*? I think we've probably bested the Magnanos, who have only *done* 34. And we absolutely *must* take a cruise, where we don't have to stay overnight in all those weird places and we'll be protected from foreigners."

"Oh dear." His voice grew small.

"I don't think I can take it, Mark. I really don't."

"Hang in there, Babe. I'm calling with some great news that I hope will make it all worthwhile."

Gloria sighed. "I could sure use some good news."

"Do you remember me talking about two talented women I used to write stories with, a long time ago, back when I thought I could become a writer?"

"Hmm. Rings a bell I suppose. Why?"

"Well, I bumped into them at the St Louis airport, and guess what?"

Gloria sat down on the sofa. "Mark, I'm in no mood for guessing games."

"They have become ghost writers for some French novelist, and they are making a killing."

"That's nice Mark."

"No, no listen. Here's the great news I was referring to. They are making so much money that they bought a French island in the Caribbean. It's Petit Cayman. They own the whole island!"

"Well, good for them." Another sip of wine.

Mark, slightly louder and at a faster pace, continued. "Babe, the island is 95% wildlife preserve and the other 5% is the Southern Cross Club, an exclusive retreat for Europe's rich and famous, and you're not going to believe this..."

"Mark," Gloria said, eyes closed to keep the pounding headache at bay, "I'm really not..."

"Please Gloria, let me finish. After a few drinks they told me they were looking for an Executive Director and CFO for the club, because the former couple who held the job have retired, and they are looking for a mature couple with no real ties to the U.S. to fill the roles. So, I said, I thought you and I could do the job and they wholeheartedly agreed."

Gloria jumped to her feet. The headache suddenly subsided. "What did you just say?"

"The job is little more than making sure the whole club runs smoothly. They've already got a cook and a dive master and a housekeeper and a bar tender and a landscaper. Our job would be to order supplies as needed and make our guests feel comfortable. And get this; we get a fat slice of the profits, a bungalow, access to all the amenities, two months off to come back to the states and..."

"But, but, Mark." Gloria began pacing. "We just moved here and..."

"So, we sell the place. At a loss if need be. Who cares? We've got everything we need and big fat 401K's. The realtor said he could move it quickly if we ever wanted."

Gloria opened her mouth to speak but nothing came out.

"Look," Mark pleaded. "We always said we needed to add more spontaneity to our lives. Here's our chance. What have we got to lose? If we hate it, we move back to another manor house in some other neighborhood. No harm done."

"Mark," Gloria said. "I'm not a young woman anymore."

"So?"

"In case you haven't noticed, I'm a bit saggy. And this is a French resort. There's going to be plenty of fine scenery running around and..."

"WHAT? You're worried about saggy boobs? I love you just the way you are. And by the way, have you taken a good look at me lately? I'm looking more like elephant man with each passing day." He paused, then evenly, earnestly, continued. "Look, Gloria, I know several excellent surgeons who'll give you the world's best boob job."

A long pause.

"Gloria?" Mark said. "I really want this." He went on and on about fresh seafood daily and Magnificent Frigate birds and million-dollar sunsets. Gloria looked out her front window. Candace and that self-absorbed Magnano woman, illuminated by the full moon, were striding up her walkway. They each carried a wine bottle in one hand, and a wine glass in the other.

"Mark," she interrupted. "Hold it right there. I'm sold. Gotta go. I've got packing to do."

*Donna's Comments: This started out as a rather serious and judgmental piece. Sue took it to a more light-hearted direction, and I certainly did not see the ending coming. Amazing where three brains can go!*

*Sue's Comments: Donna set us up with a character who was ripe for satire, and I couldn't resist poking fun at people who have traveled widely and still managed to avoid learning anything new, and how many countries they have done is just another notch on their status symbol belt. I loved Alan's resolution.*

*Alan's Comments: My contribution was easy to write as I had always dreamed of running the Southern Cross Club on Little Cayman Island. I don't know if it still exists, but it was quite a place. One of the benefits of writing stories is it doesn't matter if they were a dream and the premise really doesn't make sense. Who cares? It's my dream and I love it!*

# FINAL SHOT

## By Donna, Alan, Sue

The silver-haired socialite grasped her lipstick with perfectly manicured fingers, poised and ready for her visitors. Matilda tottered in wearing a crisp white blouse, tucked carefully into her substantial waistband, black skirt barely covering abundant knees.

"Miz von Schilling, one of the gentlemen here. He want to set up his 'quipment. Okay I let him into the liberry?"

"Of course, Matilda. Please show him in. Make sure he knows I'll be sitting in the armchair in front of the bay window, in the liBRARy. I want the gardens in the background. I'll be right in."

"Yes'm."

The cameraman fumbled with his tripod and tried to position the lights on either side of her designated chair. "Damn thing looks like a throne," he mumbled. "Didn't know there were any chairs like this anymore, outside of castles, anyway."

"Talking to yourself, young man? Some say that's a sign of deep intelligence...or complete insanity. I'm not sure which. What do you say?"

He straightened himself and struggled with his shirttail, immediately feeling underdressed in jeans and a denim shirt. The lady seemed to glide across the shiny oak floors and sit gracefully, her violet eyes brightening the room. She tilted her head, urging an answer to her question.

"Oh, uh, I'm just the photographer. Mr. Braxton is running late. He's the person coming to interview you. I'm just the photographer," he repeated.

"But you can speak, I hear. So, intelligent or insane? And don't you dare say you are JUST a photographer again. That's denigrating. Don't you like yourself? Don't you think this upcoming story about me would be woefully dull without pictures, young man? And what is your name?"

Oh, jeez, he thought. Where is Braxton? He adjusted the tripod a few inches higher, surprised at how tall the old lady was, sitting in that throne-like chair with such ease.

"I'm Roger, ma'am. Let me get this focused." He peered through the lens and saw a captivating woman. Staring into her eyes through the camera, as she stared back, made Roger lose track of time. He imagined what a looker she must have been in her day and could almost picture her manicured hands slipping a slender cigarette into an ivory and diamond holder, waiting for him to light it. Her deep gravelly voice ensured a smoking history, and he wondered if she missed it.

"I can tell you're not much of a talker. Guess that's why you hide behind the camera." She shifted slightly, touching the pearls at her neck and smoothing a bejeweled hand across the cornflower blue chiffon lap. "Have you ever visited Champlain Gardens before, Roger? I assume you have a last name." She persisted, with a piercing smile.

"No, ma'am. First time. Last name's Broadfield." He was not expecting to be chatted up by this rich old lady. All he wanted to do was take a few pictures and call it a day. Where was that damn Braxton?

"Oh. Roger Broadfield. Are you any relation to Reginald Broadfield with Global Publishing? Is he, was he, your grandfather? You look like him, except for the long hair. His was curly, too, but of course back then people got regular haircuts." She laughed, just slightly, just enough that he wouldn't feel insulted.

"Yes. I am the grandson of the infamous Reginald Broadfield." Please don't ask me any more personal questions, he begged silently. He wanted to repeat that he was just a photographer but bit his tongue.

"Hmph. I have the best view of any in this building. Don't you agree? The scarlet tulips and golden petunias greet me every afternoon when I take my stroll. Do you stroll, Roger? Your grandfather liked to stroll, but of course I didn't live here when I knew him. I was relegated here with the rest of the rich old people who vacillate between intelligent and insane, which brings us back to my original question."

Oh, God, save me from this, please, he thought. Where is that damned Braxton?

Matilda appeared at the library door, carrying a silver tray. "Scuze me, Miz von Schilling. A Mr. Braxton called to say he was stuck in traffic and would be another twenty-thirty minutes, so I thought you and your guest would prolly want some refreshment."

"Perfect timing, 'Tilly. I think Mr. Broadfield would

proBABly welcome an excuse not to talk. Bring it in, please." She patted her cottony hair and stood, floating toward the sofa near the fireplace. "While we're waiting, would you like to know how I know your grandfather?" Her eyes twinkled, and Roger knew he would hear the story whether he wanted to or not.

Shoulders sagging, Roger slunk into an overstuffed leather chair, across from where Miz von Schilling sat. "Oh, come now, Roger. It's not *that* bad. You're not being punished. I would think you'd want to know some family history."

"Ma'am, I need to tell you. I don't feel too kindly about my grandfather. He never had no time for my momma and sisters. We were, in his eyes, the black sheep of the family."

Miz von Schilling smiled, holding her teacup in both hands. "He could be irascible, no denying. And when he made up his mind, there was no changing it. But his contributions changed our lives. I'm not talking about his publishing company. I'm referring to other work he did, we did, that made a huge difference."

Roger shrugged again. Come on Braxton.

"Our time together was brief. Long before the passing years finally caught up with us. We were both young and full of vigor. Idealistic, would be the word that described us. Your grandfather was a journalist back then, covering whatever stories that might sell a newspaper."

She put down her teacup, paused, then said, "And I, young man, was a German spy."

In the silence that followed, Roger sat back in his chair, studying the face of the woman seated across the room. Is she for real?

"I can see by the surprise on your face that you didn't know that did you? That's okay. I haven't started owning up to my past until recently. I doubt if the authorities will take me away and shoot me at my age."

"Whatever you say, ma'am."

She smiled again. "And your grandfather provided me with a steady stream of information for my employer, Kaiser Wilhelm II. He was a pacifist and wanted to keep your country out of the war in Europe, so he was perfectly willing to slip me updates regarding the continued discord between congress and your president. This in turn, encouraged the Germans to keep the pressure on France and England, knowing that the Americans were not ready. Then came the sinking of the Lusitania by a German submarine, and that changed everything."

Roger said nothing but continued to stare. Yeah, sure lady. And I'm the Easter Bunny. He glanced at his watch. These crazy old people are driving me nuts. I've got to find another gig. Come on Braxton.

"He was crushed by the turn of events. Beneath his crusty exterior, there was a man of great passion. For a time, we spoke of moving to Paris after the war, and trying our hand at writing. You see, I too dreamed of writing my own novel."

More silence.

"I suspect by the time you met him, he was a shell of his former self, worn down by life and all its disappointments. If the first world war took away some of his zeal, the second war destroyed him."

She sipped her tea. "But there was a time...back before it all the madness...those were exciting days." Her gaze drifted off to a time and place long forgotten.

"We were also lovers."

An image of this old broad lying naked and inviting on a bed flashed before his photographer's eyes, and he squeezed them tightly to dispel it as quickly as possible.

"Roger," her voice came to him through a fog. She chuckled. "I know, you young people can't imagine us old folks ever being young and idealistic – and sex-driven. But it happens to everyone, even you – the getting old part, not necessarily the sex part."

She drifted off, focusing on something only she could see. "Oh my, we were something together. He knew just what I wanted and, oh my goodness, could he deliver."

This was way more information than Roger, even in his most absurd fantasy, ever wanted. His grandfather "delivering"? Gross! Where the hell was Braxton? He was going to have to pay him extra for this gig.

To give himself a moment to reorient himself, he tossed a crustless (and tasteless) cucumber sandwich into his mouth and washed it down with a swig of tea. Then he looked over at the old lady, who was still meandering down memory lane, uninterested, for the moment, in making small talk.

In that moment, he saw her with new eyes. Usually, he got a kick out of photographing old people – at least quiet old people. Their wrinkled faces and withered bodies made them far more interesting subjects than your average young or middle-aged person, kind of like a weathered old barn, with a few boards missing and the doors hanging from the hinges told a much better story than a shiny new one.

But as he looked at Miz von Schilling, lost in her

reverie, he saw something more. Beneath the carefully applied make-up, he discerned a glow; her eyes sparkled with youthful exuberance, and her body relaxed. She was transformed. Damn! He wished he had his camera on her right now; it would be a prize-winner for sure. He started to reach for it surreptitiously.

The moment was lost when Matilda opened the door and said, "Mr. Braxton. He here now, ma'am."

Roger sighed as he watched his chance for a Pulitzer slip away. Miz von Schiller straightened up and said, "Show him in, Matilda."

Braxton entered, scattering his apologies for being late, looked over at the woman reclining regally on the sofa and said, "Eugenie! My god, I swear you haven't changed a bit in 50 years. As beguiling as ever."

She stood to greet him. "Braxton, you old goat. Still piling on the malarkey." They both laughed. She opened up her arms and they shared a kiss that had far more fire than the typical "old friends" greeting.

"Holy shit!" thought Roger. "Who the hell is this woman?"

*Donna's comments: This started from a photo prompt in our Writers' Guild, as I was pressed to produce something within our "Hot Potatoes" timeline.*

*Alan's comments: Can you imagine! Here you are, photographing some old lady when first you discover she had a love affair with your dreadful grandfather, and then you learn they were connected in some sort of spy ring! Wouldn't that simply be the most fascinating day of your entire career? Who would believe it?*

*Sue's comments: I had great fun with this one. I loved the character Donna and Alan handed me.*

# Ripples

By Sue, Donna, Alan

G ray clouds hung heavy on the pond. The air was still; nothing moved. No birds flitted from tree to tree; a turtle had crawled halfway out of the water and then stopped, too lethargic to bother either hoisting himself onto the shore or slipping back into the water. Even the fish swam in lazy circles, uninterested in the mosquitos that hovered above them. A young girl, maybe thirteen or fourteen, sat by the edge of the water, as immobile as the scene around her.

She reached toward the rocky shore, picked up a pebble, and tossed it into the water. She watched as the ripples spread slowly, evenly across the surface, creating a small fluttering of the reeds over to her left. She picked up another, slightly larger, and threw it with more force to see if the ripples would reach the far side of the pond. Then she tried a whole handful of pebbles, roiling the water and causing the turtle to lift its head and look languidly around before settling back. Finally, she grabbed a large rock, and lifting it over head with two hands, plunged it into the water. She jumped back to avoid getting soaked and noticed that the ripples spreading out were rough, uneven, graceless, and had startled the turtle, the fish, and even the birds.

She sat back down and smiled ruefully, hearing her grandmother's voice as she slipped in to comfort her after her father had yet again sent to her bedroom for talking back and making a scene. "Maggie, my girl," she'd whisper, stroking her hair, "easy, easy. Quiet speaks louder than noise; gentle is stronger than harsh. The small act of kindness is more powerful than the brash act of anger. Don't let him get to you. Fight back with silence and a smile, and the knowledge that you are right – when you are. Of course, that's not always the case, and then just take your medicine."

For almost a year now, the only place Maggie heard that gentle voice was in her head. Her grandmother's death – sudden, unexpected – had left her bereft of her guide, her comfort, her confidante, her friend. Her mother had lit out for San Francisco and freedom when Maggie was only two and never come back. Her father, angry, annoyed, and very busy making money, had turned to his mother, who had uprooted her life and come to be both mother and father to Maggie.

She picked up another pebble, tossed it into the water and watched as the ripples kept spreading until they finally petered out. Then she stood up, brushed off her rear end, and started walking slowly toward home.

The shaded path around the pond sheltered a small playground on one side and picnic tables on the other. Maggie started to avoid the chattering kids scooting up the sliding board, not in the mood for lighthearted laughter, but a sudden idea changed her mind. "When something bothers you, when you have a question, study on it," her grandmother had suggested. Study on it. That's what she would do. She would study the children and their mother, listening for answers.

"You two boys are so silly. Why struggle to go up the slide the wrong way, when you can just climb the ladder and glide down the right way?" Clearly not chiding them, the woman pushed her sunglasses to the top of her head and juggled a toy in front of the pinked-out baby propped in a stroller.

Maggie watched the infant giggle and grab at the toy, which her Mom held just out of reach. The lady leaned in to kiss both cheeks, returning her attention to her sons.

"Hey, Mommy. Know why? 'Cause it's more funner. It's more funner going *up* the slide, right, Toddy?" The younger child lost his balance and fell on his padded bottom, still in diapers. Their laughter echoed across the pond, across Maggie's heart.

Their mother strolled closer, touching the toddler's tow-headed locks. "You're taking such good care of your little brother, Max." She kissed them both and pushed the baby back to their bench.

"Hey, Mommy, look at this. Look at this! I'm the king and Todd is a dragon."

She gave them a thumbs up and smiled.

That's how it's supposed to be, Maggie thought, feeling a twinge of jealousy. How could a mother just leave her child? That mother would never ever leave them, never think of leaving them. That's a picture of love right there, she envied. Although her grandmother never said one negative word about Maggie's mother, she knew something was missing. Maggie wished she had asked why her father would marry someone so mean. She must have been mean. A nice person wouldn't leave her child, just walk out and never look back.

She stood erect and determined to find the answer, to find her mother, and walked resolutely across the playground area toward home. Maggie smiled at the two little boys, waved at them and marched toward home.

Maggie knew her father wouldn't return from his golf outing until close to five o'clock. She hung her key over the foyer and relocked the door, setting the security system. I have three hours to start digging, and his closet is the first place to explore, she decided. She set the alarm on her phone and headed upstairs. Then had one more thought.

*"Dad, I'm fixing supper for us tonight. Can you please let me know when you're on the way home?"* she texted. "He will be shocked, I'm sure." Maggie could hear her Grandmother reminding her, "You can catch more flies with honey than you can with vinegar."

The girl could barely reach a lidded box on the top shelf of his closet, glad it wasn't heavy. She just knew it would have some papers, maybe letters, maybe pictures, something that would lead to her mother's whereabouts. She'd never been happier when she lifted the lid.

(Thirteen years later)

The PBS interviewer began, "Tonight's feature is a heartwarming success story. I'm standing on the sidewalk in front of *Ripples: A Safe Place for Children*. This was once a run-down store in a run-down block of a run-down city and now, it is an award-winning, creative haven for children who need, well, a safe place to work out their issues. This is accomplished by a process known as Play Therapy. When *Ripples* opened their doors four years ago, local officials and community leaders had little hope of their survival. How wrong they were! Now, *Ripples* has three locations throughout the city, all filled to capacity, making a huge difference in places that at one time, had little hope. The "big wins," as the owners Karen and Maggie call them, are too numerous to list. And take a look around." The camera person scanned the neighborhood. "As if taking its cue from *Ripples*, this corner of town has seen a cultural renaissance and is now burgeoning with art studios, book shops, great smelling bakeries, and inviting coffee shops. These are the stories we love to report. Now, let's go in and meet the owners."

He turned and walked in; the camera person following, filming every step. Two women rose from where they sat on a leather sofa and shook hands with him.

The interviewer began. "Thanks for agreeing to be our feature story."

He faced the camera. "Let me introduce you to the owners of *Ripples*; Karen Smith age 29, and her younger sister, Maggie Pascucci, age 26."

The camera turned back to the women.

"Let's get right to it," he began. "You've accomplished what most experts said was impossible. You started with a dream and a small business loan, and never looked back. Your clients are children, many deeply troubled, and your successes are now national news. Several Universities are studying your operation, in hopes of replicating this type of therapy elsewhere. I have to ask: what's your secret?"

Karen said, "No secret. Here's what we do." She launched into an explanation that if written as a recipe, would read:

- *Take a dozen damaged children,*
- *Encourage them to invent short theatrical plays,*
- *Add a make-shift small but intimate setting,*
- *Sift in heavy doses of love, compassion, kindness, and patience.*
- *Stir just until combined. Do not over mix!*
- *Repeat as necessary.*

The interviewer shook his head and smiled. "Clearly, you two are making quite a difference."

Then he turned to Maggie.

"I understand that you both went through your childhood and into your teenage years, without even knowing you had a sister. How did you finally get together after all those years?"

Maggie smiled and said, "It all started when I found a box on the top shelf of my father's closet. I took it down and lifted the lid."

*Sue's comments: I had no idea where I wanted this story to go. I was just having fun creating a mood and a moment. I love where they took it.*

*Donna's Comments: Once again, I took this as far as I could, setting up a mysterious plot, then gladly tossed it to Alan to finish.*

*Alan's comments: Again, great fun. My characters were Sue and Donna (bet you didn't guess that!) but also, my sister-in-law Karen, who in fact, works with broken people. This is precisely the type of business she could (and does) run.*

# THE EVENT

By Alan, Sue, Donna

*Note: The idea for the following short story was shame-lessly lifted from "The Kiss" by Anton Chekhov.*

It was in fact, truly a dark and stormy night. Wave after wave of thunderstorms rolled through. The lights had already gone out (and then back on) twice, and the way they were flickering, it was about to happen again. Nonetheless, the Post-Pandemic party kept on. Almost a year of stress, fear, and anger was dissipating with the liberal flow of wine and beer. The over-sized gathering, stuffed indoors at an acquaintance's Manor house due to the off and on downpours, was undeterred in their merrymaking. Social distancing was now a thing of the past and nary a mask could be found. Voices and laughter were loud, and the scorching humidity – untouched by the non-functioning AC unit - hardly dented the enthusiasm.

I was approaching a critical crossroad. Having downed three beers already, I knew from seventy years

of experience that I stood on that all too familiar preci-
pice: if I kept drinking, my IQ would plummet, and dire
consequences could indeed follow. If I quit now and
changed to tonic water, I might survive the night without jamming my size 12 foot into my big mouth. Hmm.
Quite a decision. But first, I was in pressing need of a
commode. The decision would have to wait.

The front bathroom was occupied, so I headed
down a long hallway, past the spare bedroom, to the
guest bath. Just as I arrived, the lights winked out
again. Fortunately, some considerate soul had lit a can-
dle which was flickering on the back of the toilet. Good
thing. My aim was true, no mess no fuss.

On my way out, I started down the pitch-black hall
toward the candle-lit party room. Then it happened. As
I walked past the spare bedroom, a hand reached out
from the inky darkness, grabbed my arm and pulled
me into the room. Then, a woman – and yes, I'm sure it
was a woman – wrapped her arms around my neck and
planted a wet, energetic, fervent kiss onto my lips. She
pressed her body against mine in a most alluring way,
and then was gone. Upon being released, I staggered
back a step or two, and said, "What the fuck?"

Regaining at least some of my composure, I felt my
way out of the abject darkness and headed toward the
party at the end of the hallway. As I entered the room,
the lights came back on, greeted by a resounding cheer
by the merry makers. Blinking in the bright light, I
searched the faces of all partiers: nothing. There was
no sly smile, no wink, no nothing.

I just stood there, mumbling, "What the fuck?"

Although I knew most of the attendees – some very

well – there were a few newbies, friends, or relatives of our neighbors, all eager to finally be free to laugh, love, and be merry, throwing caution to the winds.

But who here was so emboldened as to break pretty solid social taboos and throw herself shamelessly into the arms of a married man? Not that we were a prudish community – far from it, at least according to the ever-grinding rumor mill. But holy shit, this was a mystery worthy of my alter-ego, Hercule Poirot. As any good sleuth does, I began by laying out the possibilities and decided that it was A) the act of some love-starved hoyden, B) somebody pulling my leg, C) somebody who had way more than three beers, or D) the figment of my supercharged imagination.

I methodically set about assessing each of the options. I began by appraising the female occupants of the room to see if any might fit the first category, beginning with the ones I didn't know. My initial scan failed to produce any likely suspects: they were a very ordinary-looking group of senior citizens (God! I hate that term!) standing or sitting, chatting pleasantly.

But then I noticed one woman standing over by the window, looking out at the storm-tossed trees. She was set apart by her appearance as well – a drab gray dress that hung loosely, but still managed to reveal a body shapelier than those of her peers; her silver-streaked black hair pulled severely back into a twist, accentuating high cheek bones and, at least from a distance, a relatively wrinkle-free face.

Could she be the one? I reached for another beer. What the hell. In for a dime; in for a dollar. Now that I think about it, I think I vaguely remember her staring at me earlier. She couldn't possibly know that Carrie and

I have been sleeping in separate bedrooms for several months – yet another relationship whose tenuousness has been laid bare by pandemic-enforced proximity. I'm sure *nobody* knows about us, although I do have my suspicions about Jane and Don.

Okay. Category A gets a "Possible." I took several swigs of my Corona (a clever ironic touch of our hosts), proud of my sleuthing skills so far. What about category B? No shortage of candidates here, though most of them are male, and even in drag in a pitch-dark room they couldn't pass muster – scratchy faces, hairy arms, pot bellies. Nope, not them. But what about some of the women – Marilyn, Irene, or maybe Carolyn – she never misses a chance to pull my chain. Nah. Even though I've never experienced their bodies plastered suggestively against mine, I'm pretty sure I'd know.

Hmm. That leaves C or D. This is going to take another beer.

Using the process of elimination, I tossed Category B aside, since any pranksters I knew would be unable to hide their obvious glee at having pulled one over on me. Scanning the room, sucking on beer number five I searched for any clearly inebriated female who was well put-together. The large room, packed beyond sensible capacity, made the search difficult without moving around, so I forced myself to move into the mayhem.

Narrowing down my choices seemed easy, since few of the women were as well-built as the one who had pressed against me, and the few who were hung onto a mate for drunken stability. I picked my way through screaming clusters of vaccinated celebrants, some trying to dance to the music that had just blasted back on.

There, half-sliding down the lone fireside armchair, I spotted a black silk dress wrapped around a long-legged body. Could she have been the one who grabbed me, kissed me and returned ahead of me to such an inebriated state? I'll explore.

"Excuse me. Are you alone?" What kind of question is that? A pick-up line from a seventy-year-old married man?

"Wha—wha'd you say? Do I know you? Who are you?" She tried, and failed, to slide back up to a sitting position.

I seemed to have surprised her from a drunken stupor. This could not have been the woman who planted a big one on me in the dark. Nevertheless... "I'm Mark. Mark Slater. You looked like, uh, you needed help."

"I'm taking a nap. No help needed. And yes, I am alone, happily. A better question might be why I am here."

Her melodic voice soothed my soul. She didn't sound annoyed, just matter-of-fact. Not drunk, just sleepy. This was a good sign, except that I couldn't wrap my head around how she could have gotten out of that guest bedroom and across this packed space without my having seen her.

Category D is creeping into the realm of possibility. Did someone, an oversexed woman, really grab me in the black-out, or had it been a figment of my imagination? I put my fifth beer down on the mantle and stared at her.

"Did you, uh, have you wandered around this house? I mean, what did you do when all the lights went out?"

"The lights went out? How would I know? I've been sleeping."

I scanned the room to see if anyone noticed me talking to this beautiful woman in the sexy black dress. Where were Don and Jane, suspicious that my marriage wasn't as happy as theirs? Speaking of which, where was my wife? Hadn't seen her since the first black-out.

She worked her way around the maze of people, like a trained mouse, carrying two glasses. "Are you still drinking beer, or do you want to try one of these cocktails? Where have you been, anyway? Have you met any new people?"

My wife looked pretty good in her white pantsuit. Not many broads her age, our age, could sport that out-fit. Well, maybe it was the booze.

"As a matter of fact, I have met someone." I turned to introduce the unnamed sleeper in the silky black dress. The empty armchair invited me to sit by the fire.

"What the fuck?" I mumbled.

*Alan's comments: I have always loved The Kiss by Anton Chekhov. Can you imagine? What would you do? And maybe the most fun of all was watching Sue and Donna try to figure out what to do with this. To their credit, they did a terrific job!*

*Sue's comments: What the heck was I going to do with this one? I was a 70-year-old man who had just re-lieved himself in the dark and was accosted by some-one who laid a big kiss on him??? Once again, I just started writing and handed it off to Donna when I was running out of ideas.*

*Donna's comments: What fun. Another one out of my comfort zone. I amazed myself with a decent ending, just letting my imagination go where parts one and two led me.*

# THE TAILOR

By Donna, Alan, Sue

They could have been brothers, although one clearly took better care of himself. Both wore black suits and Stetson hats much like the President. The larger man sat uncomfortably on the edge of the metal bench, jacket unbuttoned out of necessity and tie loosened for the same reason. His partner resembled his younger self, trim in his well-tailored suit, crisp white shirt and tie knotted perfectly at his neck. They waited and watched for their target.

"Think he'll even show up?" the heavy man asked. "I'm betting he won't."

"If I were a betting man, I would win. He's already here. See, over there, feeding the pigeons."

Pulling his tie tighter, he glanced ever so slightly toward the flock of pigeons on the other side of the park. "You're kidding me. That guy? No way."

The younger man pulled an unfiltered Camel out of the pack, lit it slowly, and threw the match on the sidewalk. "Frank, it's a wonder you ever qualified for this service. You are such a bad judge of weapons. Look at him and tell me what you see."

"Humph. Been around longer than you, Leo. Who

do you think hired you? Anyway, here's what I see...a dapper gentleman dressed too nicely not to be noticed. I mean, look at those shoes. What are they, spats? Anybody see him doing something suspicious and the first thing they would do is describe a sharp-dressed gentleman wearing fancy shoes and a hat that looks like it had been made by the President himself."

"Exactly. And who in his right mind would give him a second thought if the word 'spy' came into the conversation? He's too obvious, garners attention immediately, and therefore, my friend, is a perfect candidate. Besides, Harry himself recommended him for the job."

Frank eyed his partner, then looked again at the pigeon-feeding gentleman. "Well, he did show up. He must be interested and willing to see what's going on."

They observed the dapper man standing alone with an open bag of breadcrumbs, just as the note had instructed him to do. He'd found it folded in the cuff of the suit pants he was shortening. *"Feed the pigeons at exactly 3:22 tomorrow."*

Rob knew immediately that his old friend Harry needed him and his heart quickened. He folded the paper and stuck it in his slacks, smoothed it flat, and returned to pinning the cuffs. He knew the war was not over by a long shot and he was glad to serve. Damn commies, he thought.

So now he would wait and watch. The two matching suits across the park must be his contacts. So obvious, Rob thought. Guess I'll feed the pigeons until they come to me. Who could be watching? What could he do to help the cause? To help his friend?

The thinner, well-dressed man approached from

his left before Rob even realized he had gotten up from the bench. Tipping his hat, he asked, "Got a light?"

That was the code passed to him in the jacket brought in last evening, just before he closed the shop. That's all it said. *Got a light?* The customer said he just needed to fix the lining and she would get it tomorrow at exactly 3:00. She stressed "exactly" and looked straight into his eyes. Rob understood and searched all the pockets before hanging the suit coat on the next day's repair rack.

Rob Fleming had turned out the lights in his tailor shop, flipped the sign from OPEN to CLOSED, and locked the door. He pulled the brim on his Stetson slightly down over his right eye and took a deep breath. The fresh spring air boosted his spirits as he strolled two blocks to his apartment on F Street. There was no question that he would get very little sleep before his meeting the next day.

And now, here he was, ready to participate in some espionage that would hopefully ruin some communists. Rob pulled out his matchbook and lit the stranger's cigarette. "How can I help?" he asked, whispering, not sure if he should say anything. The man tipped his hat again and walked away, right past the other fellow he had just been sitting with.

"Say," said the heavyset man, "do you know a good tailor around? I need to bring in a few things to get altered, you know, maybe loosen the waist, move some buttons, that kinda thing."

Fleming made a face, looking puzzled. "I'm a tailor—"

The large man grabbed the tailor's shoulder in a friendly way. "Son of a gun! I bet you do good work, right? Always pick the sharpest looking guy to get good advice. You're a tailor? Son of a gun! Always check the pockets, huh?" He offered a hearty laugh and clapped Fleming's shoulder again.

He lumbered off like a grizzly—big, burly and confident.

The following morning Rob Fleming strolled to his shop at precisely 9 AM, just as he had for the last six years. He and Harry had been in the trenches together and had become great friends once they learned of each other's previous lives, Harry a haberdasher and Rob a floundering clothes designer. The depression ruined Rob's attempts to succeed in New York and he eventually returned to his mother's home in Virginia. Harry's shining star rose, however, and after his election and move to Washington, D.C., he looked up his old friend and encouraged him to open a shop in the country's capital.

"Come on up here, Robbie," Harry implored him. "The post war men around here are in desperate need of a good tailor. All they know is uniforms!"

And now, Rob realized, his old friend had "hired" him as a spy. The familiar female customer came in shortly after he flipped his sign to OPEN. She handed over two shirts and asked if he could adjust the wrist buttons to accommodate cuff links.

"Of course," Rob replied. "How soon do you need them?"

"Three o'clock tomorrow. Thank you." The tailor noted her slim waist, accented with a small leather belt, and her shapely legs atop the nylons and high heels. He returned the smile her red lips had sent his way.

But first, Rob had to check the pockets and all the seams and get ready for the next customer.

Try as he would, Rob couldn't shake the vision of her red lips all day. But business was brisk, and he busied himself in his work. Finally, well after closing, Rob focused upon the two shirts she had dropped off. Holding his breath, hands trembling, he searched the seams and pockets for some sort of note but found nothing.

At precisely three PM the next day, Miss Red Lips came through the door. Rob handed over the shirts – she looked at the cuffs and approved of the modifications – then she turned to leave. But she stopped, with her hand on the doorknob, and turned.

"Excuse me," she asked. "Do you know how to get rid of moles?"

"Moles?"

"Yes, I believe we have a mole or perhaps moles, in our flowers. They seem to be particularly fond of the roses."

"Well," Rob began, blinking away the obvious surprise and confusion. "There's a hardware store two blocks to the north..."

But she turned and left before he finished.

Rob stood frozen, watching her walk away.

Closing was five minutes away when the bell above the door tinkled. Rob swore to himself. It had been a jangling, unnerving day. All he wanted to do was go home. But he put on his 'patron friendly' face and moved to the counter to greet the customer.

A frumpy, overweight, disheveled women stood, her arms wrapped around a large sack.

"May I help you?"

She plopped the laundry bag down on the counter, exhaled, and stepped back. "Sorry to drop in so late in the day but my bosses are so disorganized they only know their names because people are always yelling them at them and that's 'cause they can't figure out..."

Rob held up his hand and smiled. "So how may I help you?"

"They want us to change all the buttons, they do. Can't be brass anymore, they say. Must be silver-colored. In keeping with those crazy politicians and they keep changin' their minds about what image they need to project because..."

Rob held up his hand again. "Slow down. Now, from the top. Who are you?"

"I'm Ethel Jameson I am, and for the last four years I've been handlin' all the domestic duties..."

Rob took out an order form. "Okay Ethel. Now, what is it you'd like to me to do?"

"They came to me late in the day. I'm supposed to be home fixin' dinner for my Jamie but no-o-o, this has to be done right away..."

Rob smiled patiently. "And what is that?"

"Why," she said, "all the buttons on all the coats have to be changed to silver of course. Now mind you, there's nothin' wrong with the brass..."

"Okay," Rob said. "Let me write this down. *Change all buttons to silver*. This should be easy enough. I believe I can get this done by the end of the week."

"And there'll be more 'cause they didn't want to go without coats for even a day, those stuffed shirts, they always have to..."

Rob took more notes. "Got it. More to follow. I'll

make sure I have enough silver buttons. Now, how can
I reach you when the job is done?"

"Just call me and I'll come right over."

"Okay," Rob said. "Call when complete. And a phone
number where I can reach you?"

"Oh," she said, screwing up her face. "I don't rightly
know. Just call and ask for Ethel. They'll know how to
fetch me."

Patiently, Rob asked, "And who should I call?"

"Why, the Soviet Embassy of course."

Closing time or no closing time, Rob needed to sit
and sort things out. He turned out the lights, flipped
the sign to CLOSED, and went back into his small office. He was happy to think he could help out his old
buddy Harry, who had his hands full running a country
that was still reeling from a World War and gearing up
to face a far more subtle enemy. But Holy Cow! This
spy business was really confusing.

He took out the pad he used for the notes and
sketches for his alterations and started writing.

- *People*
- *Fat Guy – check the pockets*
- *Cigarette Man – Got a light?*
- *Red Lips – moles? What the hell does that mean?*
- *Ethel Yappy Lady – Silver buttons – Soviet Embassy*

Rob studied his notes and shook his head. He
couldn't make any more sense of the whole spy thing
now than he had before. He kept circling back to Red

Lips, both because she was, well, Red Lips and very attractive, and because of her seemingly irrelevant comment about moles. In this strange time after the war, in what had come to be known as the Cold War, it seemed like it was a battle of spies, and he had been recruited to their ranks. Somewhere in the back of his brain, he remembered hearing about moles, who were kind of double agents, spies who passed on the information to the enemy.

So, if that was the case, who was the mole? He looked again at his list. Fat Guy and Cigarette Man seemed to be a pair, so not likely that one was a mole. Red Lips wouldn't warn about moles if she *was* one. So that left Yappy Ethel, who didn't seem to have the wits to be a spy, let alone a mole. What to do? What to do?

He got up and began to pace but quickly found that pacing in his tiny office was seriously curtailed. Two steps in any direction brought him to a wall, window, desk, or door. It nonetheless yielded fruit quickly and he called out loud, "Check the pockets!"

He went back out into the store and started going through the pockets in the bag of coats Ethel had dumped on him 5 minutes before closing.

"There must be something here," he muttered as he took out each jacket and carefully checked each pocket. His initial excitement soon flagged as pocket after pocket turned up empty.

He was about to give up in despair when he remembered what he was supposed to do – change the buttons. Was it possible that the secret was in the buttons? He tapped each button on the first coat he held up. The third one sounded different – a little hollow. With trembling hands, he fiddled with the button. The top came off and a small piece of paper carefully folded popped out. He tried to make out what it said, but it seemed to be in some kind of code.

His heart sank when he saw how many jackets and how many more buttons he would have to check out. Then he realized that he was perfectly backlit by the light from his office – in full view of anyone standing outside. He definitely needed to up his game if he was going to be in this spy business, so he quickly gathered up the coats and retreated to his office.

His search turned up several more papers in code and four that he could read. One said, "3 o'clock," another said, "I'm very disappointed," a third said, "It's OK," and the fourth said, "Beware cigarettes."

Rob flattened out all the papers, stowed them carefully in his wallet, closed up the store, and went home. But sleep was not likely to come any time soon. He tossed and turned, trying to figure out who was who and what was what.

The next day, Rob set about changing the buttons, but what should have been a routine task became burdensome. He kept looking up at the clock as it crept through the day, and his fingers fumbled. He dropped buttons, pricked his fingers, and tangled the thread. At three o'clock, the bell over the door rang, and Red Lips walked in, carrying the same shirts he had fixed for her the day before.

He looked up into the striking blue eyes that held his and seemed to pierce him. "I'm very disappointed," she said, pausing, still holding his gaze. Cufflinks do not work right at all. I think I'd prefer silver buttons." She reached into her purse and handed him a packet. "I happen to have a collection here. I trust you can find the perfect match among them. You might as well keep the rest. I'm sure that in your line of work, you can put them to good use. I'll pick up the shirts tomorrow."

He started to protest, then pulled back.

"Perhaps," she continued, "in payment, you might have some small scraps," she paused "of fabric, that is. I'm working on a quilt. Would that be okay?"

"Um, yeah." His tongue got all twisted up. "It's okay."

She fixed him with a magnificent red-lipped smile and winked. "I'll wait until you get me what I need."

He was trembling as he stepped into his office. He took a deep breath and thought, *She's the one I'm supposed to give the papers to. She has to be. But what if she's the mole? I could be giving state secrets to the commies.* He reached for his wallet, then brought his hand back, the sweat beading on his forehead and running down his face.

He heard a cough from the other room, a signal to hurry up. He grabbed an envelope, put the papers into it and sealed it; then he went over to his bin of scrap fabric, filled a bag, stuffed the envelope into it, and rushed back out. She was staring out the window.

"Here you go, Miss . . ."

She ignored the hint to reveal her name, gave him her million-dollar smile, took the bag, and left, leaving him wide-eyed, sweat-stained, and totally befuddled.

A few minutes later, the bell jangled again and in walked Fat Guy and Cigarette Man. They smiled, exchanged pleasantries and walked around the shop.

Cigarette man strolled over to him, took out his pack of Camels, casually removed one, tapped it on the pack, held it out in front of him, studying it. "Got a light?" he asked.

Rob lit the cigarette with shaking hands.

Fat Guy said, "Interesting shop you have here. Do you have anything for me?"

"No, I'm sorry," he responded hesitantly. "I have only a few ready-made items here, as you can see. But I'd be happy to make something for you."

"I'm disappointed," he responded. "I thought you might have something for me – for us."

*Oh shit!* Rob thought. *I really screwed up! They're the ones I was supposed to give the papers to.*

"Yeah, I'm disappointed too," said Cigarette Man as he and his Camel got dangerously close to a suit Rob had just finished working on.

"Be careful with that cigarette!" he called, and the fourth message resonated – *Beware cigarettes.* He took a deep breath. *So maybe they must be the moles. It's not red lips.* He smiled, thinking of a future relationship with her.

His moment of bliss was short-lived. "We'll be back tomorrow," said fat guy. "I assume you'll have something for us then."

*Oh man! This spy business is scary – REALLY scary.*

Two years later, Rob was sitting on his living room couch, watching the Evening News with John Cameron Swayze.

*And now to the top story of the night,* his calm, deep voice intoned. *A carefully orchestrated Soviet spy ring has been broken up. American Intelligence has* been able to thwart a sophisticated plot to steal our atomic secrets. Two Americans, Frank DiScala and Leo Arden have been apprehended as double agents – or in current parlance, moles – passing on top secret information to the Russians. President Truman has commended the brave men and women who work in the shadows, putting their lives on the line, so that we can all sleep safely at night.

Rob reached over and squeezed the hand of the woman sitting next to him, looked into her deep blue eyes, kissed her ruby red lips, and said, "Well, we did it!"

*Donna's Comments: The genre "assigned" here was historical fiction, another direction I rarely take. As a young girl, I used to imagine that my Grandfather was a cold war spy, because he lived alone in Washington, D.C. and worked as a tailor.*

*Alan's Comments: This was the first of our stories that I thought could be expanded into something far greater...maybe a novel. I was taken by it and sorry we had to keep it short. Maybe next time.*

*Sue's Comments: Spy stories are not a genre I have ever chosen for my writing, so it was fun to branch out and see where it would go. I think the "Two years later" ending worked all right – and also got me out of a tough spot. I had no idea where else to go.*

# EDITH

### By Alan, Sue, Donna

S nowflakes descended from the gunmetal gray sky, large and distinct enough to make an audible "hiss" when hitting the gaslights.

Edith Wilson silently watched from the backseat of the luxurious Presidential motor car: a 1917 Crane-Simplex. They were parked across from the Capitol Bakery on Massachusetts Avenue.

With eyes straight ahead, Harold, her driver, asked, "Shall I catch a cab back to the servants' quarters?"

"No, not this time," Edith replied. "Perhaps, you'd be kind enough to pass an hour or so in the bakery when my friend arrives."

"It would be my honor," he said.

*Honor? Do I deserve that word? Am I honorable?*

There was a soft rap on the window. Harold quickly got out, donned his hat, and opened the back door.

A man bent down and slid into the seat alongside Edith.

Harold closed the door, picked his way across the snow covered, slippery street, then disappeared into the bakery.

The man removed his U.S. Army officers hat, then

leaned over and kissed Edith. This kiss was soft and slow.

"And how is the First Lady?" he asked as he sat back.

Ignoring his question, she stated, "So you are going."

"I am."

"I have heard that you turned down the offer to stay on as military attaché to the French embassy."

"Yes, I did."

"Pershing is doing just fine without you."

"I am needed in France."

Silence. The snow, steadier now, continued to fall. The flakes had become smaller, more insistent.

"And you are staying with Woodrow?"

"He continues to have minor strokes, and they are becoming more frequent. His doctor told me, in confidence, that they will intensify. My role is growing in importance."

"I believe that's why we have vice presidents. Marshall can do the job." He exhaled. "And what about us?"

The silence was interrupted by a faint but audible sob.

"You have chosen to follow Pershing."

"And you have chosen to stay on as First Lady." He paused, then, "He is an old man, nearly twenty years your senior. You have already told me your intimate life is, well, isn't."

"And Pershing has many subordinates that can fix him coffee." It was Edith's turn to pause. "You have already told me he expects you to provide him with firsthand reconnaissance from the front, thus exposing yourself to hostile gun fire. Sounds to me like you are expendable."

He exhaled again. "I am a junior officer. That's what we do. Someday, I'll have junior officers to do my dirty work."

"If you live long enough."

The snow had filled the tire tracks and as it melted on the warmed vehicle, was blurring the view out the car windows.

Edith put her hand on the officer's shoulder. "When do you leave?"

"Tomorrow. I take a train to New York, then catch a steamer to France." Another pause for several beats. "And you have decided to stay by his side?"

The snow had turned the world white. The bakery windows, yellow rectangles, were disappearing.

Another faint sob. "I love you."

He reached for the door handle. "I love you. And I always will."

The officer opened the door, replaced his hat, then walked into the falling snow. Within seconds, he was gone.

With Christmas fast approaching, Edith had much to occupy her time, and she managed to push her immediate concerns about Robert to the back of her mind. Social gatherings in the White House had been put on hold since America had entered the war that spring. It would have been bad form for the heads of state to be seen indulging while the rest of the country was being turned upside down. Still, it was Christmas, and she wanted to send a positive message, a note of hope and yes, even joy, amid all the sadness. That was the essential message of Christmas, wasn't it - light amid the darkness?

She took a personal interest in decorating the traditional tree in the Blue Room, having children make ornaments to be placed on the tree and around the room, modeling the idea that decorations need not be elaborate or expensive to be meaningful.

She was standing with her secretary and friend, Amy Thompson, admiring the tree, when her husband appeared.

"What do you think, Woodrow? Does it give the right message?"

"As usual, my love, you have done a superb job. I don't know how you manage to be such a help to me and still have time for the traditional wifely duties."

He stood awkwardly for a few moments, and then said, "Amy, if you would excuse us, I'm going to commandeer my wife. I assume you can finish with the decorating."

"Of course, Mr. President. I know how valuable you find her advice." She smiled at Edith and said, "You know where to find me when you're through."

Edith walked into her husband's office, took her accustomed seat across from his desk, and waited for him to share with her his latest quandary. She missed the stolen moments with Robert - his soft kisses on her neck, the way he touched her body, igniting long dormant urges – but she loved the way she had gradually gained power with Woodrow's growing dependence on her advice. She had successfully dispatched those political hacks who sought to destroy her reputation and get her to leave him before the election, and it had given her the confidence she needed to slowly, carefully increase his trust in her, until now she often sat in on some of the discussions with his top advisors. Yes, she loved Robert, but she loved her position of power even more. She was never going to leave Woodrow for him. Still, she would have loved to have him nearby so they could continue their secret meetings, and she worried about him out there on the front line and secretly kept tabs on him. Her naïve husband had given her access to all the information she needed.

She looked over at him. He was shuffling papers, stalling before broaching his subject.

"Woodrow, are you feeling all right?" she asked. He had been looking "a little poorly," her mother might have said. He took everything so seriously. He was an academic, used to operating in a world where there was either a right or wrong answer, and he was a master debater, accustomed to convincing people of the rightness of his position. The world of politics tore him in two. He couldn't understand the compromises – moral, ethical, and practical – that were required just to stay afloat. His doctor had been trying to get him to slow down, but he felt the weight of the world.

"Yeah, I'll be fine. I'm just so thankful I have you to lean on." He looked up at her, his face drawn and haggard, his eyes watery. "So, here's the problem."

As she looked into her husband's eyes, he seemed to disappear and she saw instead the leader of the free world who was about to confide in her as never before. Edith sat upright and clasped her hands on her lap. "What is it, Mr. President?"

"I am afraid, Edith. Not of our entering the war, but of my ability to lead America through this." He watched her carefully, seeing confidence and trust in her beautiful eyes. Taking a deep breath, the man picked up a pen from the gold-trimmed wooden cup and held it as if he were going to write. His fingers shook and the pen dropped on the desk. "I am afraid I am losing my grip, Edith. Literally. I cannot hold this pen well enough to make one mark, much less write my name. I cannot sign my name."

She nodded and leaned forward slightly, urging him to continue with respectful silence.

"My eyesight is failing. Things get blurry or double. Not all the time, but often enough. I'm not afraid for myself, Edith, but I'm deeply worried about what the Germans will do if this gets out. Not to mention how my weakness might affect the European countries depending on us to help. Depending on our strength, my strength. I am becoming weak, and it could shatter the world."

"You are as strong as ever, Woodrow." He was her husband, after all, and she would not fail him now. "I am behind you and beside you and forever supportive. Now, let's put our heads together and make a plan." She stood gracefully, walked around the massive desk, and put her forehead against his. "I have an idea."

Following necessarily subdued Christmas and New Year's celebrations, the days moved along seamlessly, Edith always by her husband's side in every setting, social and political. They walked hand in hand, in part to disguise his slight tremors and also to guide him if his vision faded. Edith learned to copy her husband's signature perfectly, and all of the wartime documents were signed off in a secluded Oval Office.

At her insistence, the first family entertained Mary Pickford, Douglas Fairbanks and Charlie Chaplin in the White House, "to boost the spirit of American families"

Edith insisted. The familiar tunes of "Yankee Doodle Dandy" and "Over There" echoed from every home in the country, and the world felt comforted by Woodrow Wilson's eloquent voice in his speeches. No one understood that his beautiful wife's silent encouragement helped end the war.

Once the mental pressures of wartime decisions were over, President Wilson's secret physical failings seemed to subside, which relieved them both. But the President loved her and trusted her more than ever for her stalwart support.

The 28th President of the United States was the first to cross the Atlantic while in office, and his First Lady traveled to Europe by his side to celebrate the end of the "war to end all wars." Edith reveled in the attention she got from the Parisian press, and she inwardly congratulated herself for holding onto all the valuable jewelry her first husband had showered upon her. Being the widow of a jeweler had its advantages, and the French praised the "Lady Edith" for her good taste.

There were private moments when Edith wondered if her liaison with the junior officer at the French Embassy could be rekindled, but she satisfied herself with the charming flirtations of Prime Minister Georges Clemenceau. How many women got that level of attention?

In London, Edith stood by in Buckingham Palace when the Armistice was signed, "on the eleventh hour of the eleventh day of the eleventh month," holding her breath as the President grasped the pen and wrote his name. Uncharacteristically, he gave her a subtle wink. Later they joined King George V, Queen Mary, and Princess Mary at services in St Paul's Cathedral. Edith reflected on the beauty and grandeur surrounding her and took pride in the power she absorbed. Power, she decided, was more valuable than passion, and she settled comfortably next to the man who shared his power. Who would ever dream of spending the night in Buckingham Palace?

In Rome they met Pope Benedict XV, another first for an American President, talking to the Pope while still in office. Not terribly impressed with that liaison, Edith was more interested in the charming accent of Vittorio Emanuele, King of Italy. She imagined herself being courted by him, even as his wife sat on the other side of him during their extravagant dinner.

Edith made a lot of powerful liaisons in Europe, with Woodrow's encouragement. When they returned to the States, she continued to be her husband's primary confidante.

"Your endless fight for a League of Nations will get the best of you," she advised more than once. Failure weakened his body as well as his spirit, and Edith was not surprised when he suffered a paralytic stroke on October 2, 1919. "I will stand by you," she promised at his bedside.

Edith Bolling Galt Wilson did stand by her husband, writing letters praising his accomplishments to Prime Minister Clemenceau, King George, King Emanuele, and even the Pope, hoping they would send their support for his nomination for the Nobel Peace Prize. Indeed, his frailty was boosted with that honor as his second term neared its end.

Woodrow and Edith lived a quiet life in his retirement years, taking in an occasional movie or having lunch with friends, but he finally confided that he was "tired of swimming upstream" and died on February 3, 1924, at that time the only President buried in Washington, D.C.

Edith lived on in quiet splendor, entertaining and being entertained for decades after moving out of the White House. She maintained political and social contacts with style and grace well into her eighties and attended John F. Kennedy's Inauguration, reminding the first Catholic President that she had once "hobnobbed" with the Pope after WWI.

Had Edith not died almost exactly one year after that ceremonious event, she would certainly have thought it just that Kennedy was only the second President to be buried in Washington, D.C.

*Alan's Comments: I greatly admire Edith Wilson, and believe, as some historians maintain, she was truly our first woman president. I have no idea if she was carrying on in an extra-marital adventure, but it seemed like a creative means to get lots of information to the reader. Way to go Edith!*

*Sue's Comments: This was another genre I had never tried, though I enjoy reading historical fiction. I loved what I learned through the research necessary to write my part.*

*Donna's Comments: I had to end this one??? Research was interesting and helped me pull the plot to a somewhat credible ending.*

# Revolution

By Sue, Donna, Alan

Santiago Atitlan, Guatemala - January 1964

**M**oonlight slid down the side of the volcano and danced across the water. Maria was growing tired; she had been paddling the old dugout for almost an hour and her destination, her family's village of Santiago Atitlan, was still a good half hour away. She gave herself permission to rest, and stopped paddling, letting the boat drift slowly toward the shore. While Lake Atitlan was not as overwhelming as she had remembered it as a child, it was still an impressive body of water, capable of stirring up mighty big waves.

Tonight, however, it was mirror-calm, and it looked as if a bucketful of stars had fallen from the sky and were playing on the black curtain around her. She missed the calm beauty of her homeland: the quiet streets snaking up steep hillsides, the simple homes, the women and men both in their brilliantly embroidered clothing.

Like the first girl in many Mayan families, she had been sent off to the city when she was a young teenager to work in the homes of the wealthy and send back enough money to sustain the family and supplement the meager living they could scrape from the lands around them. Generally, if the soil had been depleted, the hills steep, and the land eroded, as it was in Santiago Atitlan, the government had allowed the peasants to keep their land. If, however, the shadow government, the United Fruit Company of the United States, thought they might be able to use it for their banana crop, it was seized and they were forced to work it for slave wages. In either case, they were unable to live without some supplemental income. So, they reluctantly sent off their first daughters.

Despite the contempt the Guatemalans had for the Mayans, whom they considered backward, dirty, and ignorant, they had a long and proud history with mystical connections to the spiritual and natural world that had resisted centuries of co-existence with other cultures. Lest those secrets be revealed by the inadvertent slip of the lip of a young girl living among the "whites," the Maria was kept from the rituals and was never privy to the ancient lore.

This Maria, Maria Costello Javierez, had played her part well. She had been placed in the home of Robert Sanders, an executive of the United Fruit Company, as a personal maid to his wife, and she had used her position to not only earn enough to help support her parents, but to glean important information. She was, in fact, a spy for the revolutionary forces.

She was coming to warn her parents that the current government, which ten years ago had displaced the democratically elected government of Jacobo Arbenz under the direct guidance of the United States' CIA and the urging of the United Fruit Company, was now engaging in a purge of revolutionary leaders. There was talk of whole villages being massacred. Her father had been one of the leaders of the October Revolution of 1944, which had unseated the brutal dictator Jorge Ubico and installed Guatemala's first democratically elected president, Juan Jose Arevalo, who had a vision of replicating the structure of the US government and the New Deal of Franklin Delano Roosevelt. Her mother had fought and planned alongside him. And as a child, Maria remembered many nights of clandestine meetings, slipping away from the advancing enemy, and a few terrifying confrontations. She may not have known the Mayan secrets, but she had rebel blood in her veins and a deep commitment to justice in her heart. She thought back to her involvement in the movement, ten years earlier.

### Antigua, Guatemala – January 1954

It was market day in Antigua. Stalls lined the streets, and the buyers, mostly women from all classes but the wealthy, wandered from stall to stall, stocking up for the week. Among them was an attractive young woman with the black hair, dark eyes, and rich brown skin of a Mayan, but taller and thinner than most, and dressed in Western clothing. She slipped among the throng, scanning the crowd. The sellers, mostly Mayan women with their bright huipils, sat beside farmers who had left their homes in surrounding villages in the early hours of the morning to drive horse and wagon, carrying their scant crops, hoping to make enough sales to keep their family afloat for one more week.

Maria spotted the man she was looking for standing near the end of the street, trying to look interested in some hand-made tools. As she walked near him, she slipped him a note and then continued on. She meandered back to a woman standing in front of a strawberry seller.

"Berries look good, don't they?" she said.

"They do indeed. A bit pricy, but worth it," the woman replied.

Maria smiled, shook hands with the woman, giving her a note as well. As she moved through the old Spanish capitol, she repeated her action three more times. Then she wandered into the park and found an unoccupied bench in the shade. An older woman in the traditional dress of Santiago Atitlan plopped down at the other end, rubbing her legs in exhaustion.

She began speaking in Kaqchikel, the language of the Mayans in the lands north of Antigua. Maria stared straight ahead, responded, then stood up, stretched, and walked on.

Later that night, Maria and those she had contacted earlier, along with a few others, filtered into the home of Juan Cordilla, a leader of the labor movement.

As the group shuffled about, sitting on stools or boxes, standing at the edges of the small room, Juan began speaking.

"You all know Maria, and most of you know that she works at the home of Robert Sanders, one of the architects of the discontent with our current government. Her credentials are impeccable: her parents, Jose David and Marta Elena Costello Javierez, distinguished themselves in the October Revolution, and periodically, she has been able to give us some very important information she has gleaned from overheard conversations. What she has to tell us tonight will send chills down our spines and convince us that our 10-year-old democratic experiment is very much under siege.

## Santiago Atitian, Guatemala - January 1964

When her dugout bumped up against the shore, Maria shook herself out of the past and began again to worry about the present and how she could help her people once again. Note-passing had worked ten years ago and although thousands of her people died in governmental genocide, her ability to warn others of the threat did save many women and children. They would have to act to resist the Guatemalan government's continued suppression, but what should that action be?

She pushed the dugout off from the shore with her oar and began paddling toward the lake's center, wishing life could be calm and peaceful as it had been for her ancestors. "How can I get my people to bring arms against the tyranny without getting caught? We need to be organized and act with one purpose—our freedom and dignity."

By the time Maria paddled into Santiago Atitlan, her plan had taken hold. She would walk into the village to her parents' home and get some rest while it was still dark. Then she would find Carolla and Louis in the village square and convince them to talk to every woman before the day ended. They had stockpiled weapons, but the attack must be timed perfectly and only the village women could get the message out.

Just as the sun began to reflect on the flat roofs and mud huts, Maria walked slowly toward the little park. She did not want to attract any attention on this Sunday morning, and knew her friends would already be awake. A small loaf of bread tucked under her colorfully embroidered shawl would suggest she was off to socialize, and any armed military should not find her presence suspicious.

"Carolla, I'm so glad to see you out and about on this beautiful morning." The girl, a bit shorter and younger than Maria, looked up from her doorway. Carolla feigned disinterest for she knew they were being watched. Always being watched. "My friend," Maria continued, "walk with me to the market. My mother wants some fish and some berries to dye her threads. She is making some beautiful pants for the holidays soon to come." She locked elbows with the girl and patted her hand.

Once they reached the dirt road leading to the park and the booths with all the goods, Carolla relaxed. Sure no one could hear them, she asked, "Do you know how much time we have? Did Sanders let anything slip out of his fat lips this week?"

"Let's find Louis in the village. I have a plan that will work if we can become good shoppers. Hurry. There isn't much time."

They found Louis squatting by his uncle's stall, stacking fruit in baskets. He seemed to be creating a food rainbow with bananas, mangoes, pineapples, and papaya next to the Nispero, Zapote Mamay, the little Jacotes, and Maria's favorite, the Maranon Jocote or Cashew Apple.

"There you are, Louis. Good to see you helping your

uncle this morning. May I suggest you put that basket of Caiminto next to the Avocado? The color contrast of purple and green will draw the attention of your customers."

Louis squinted up at his friend. If she was back in the village, then he knew she had some news. "Suggest what you want, Maria. I fill the baskets and people buy what they need. Who cares what the colors are?"

"But Louis, we are such a colorful people. It's what makes us unique. Come. Join me and Carolla over by the well. I have brought some bread. You can bring some fruit."

Stalls were beginning to get filled with goods all around the square as the three strolled over to the well. They sat on the ground and braced their backs against the stone container, facing the people and the few military strolling around.

As Maria broke the bread and handed a chunk to each of her friends, she spoke very softly. "We do not have much time. Sanders thinks 'the peasants' are planning to fight back. He is mocking the fact and bragging that we have no chance."

"So, they know we are planning a civil war?" Carolla's black eyes reflected all of their fear.

Maria bit into the Jocote, pretending to laugh. "They don't KNOW, but they sense something is up. We have to get the word out for a plan of attack before they get too suspicious. With the holidays coming up, the rich pigs will not think anything about the women of the village hanging their embroidered goods on all the stalls along the park. That is our secret weapon."

Carolla and Louis looked at their brave friend and thought she had lost her mind. What was she talking about? What did embroidery have to do with a civilian insurrection?

"Listen," Maria lowered her voice to a whisper and broke off more pieces of bread. "WE are the indigenous people. WE belong here, and we have been treated like dirt for centuries. But consider this. The Mayan language has been around for more than 5000 years, since 2000 BC. With over 800 glyphs in our language, do you think those stupid rich land grabbers have a clue? With each symbol representing a word or even a single *syllable,* there are three or four different ways to write one word."

Louis continued to look stymied, but Carolla began to smile and bit a piece of her bread. "How will we tell everyone what to write? How will we get that message out?"

"Maria," Louis cautioned, "you have told us many times about the dangers in passing notes and how close you came to getting caught ten years ago when you were just a little girl. How can we possibly—"

"Not notes, Louis," Maria interrupted. "We will get our grandmothers and mothers, our aunts and sisters to embroider a simple message for us in every piece they make and put on display. We will display the date and time of our attack throughout our village and the surrounding villages, right in front of their ignorant eyes. Our enemy may even buy the beautiful garments to take home to their wives or their girlfriends."

"Or both," Louis smiled. "I understand. I will speak to Juan Cordilla tonight and we will know what to tell every seamstress what to add to their garments. You are brilliant, my friend."

Maria grabbed another Cashew Apple and smiled for the first time in a long time.

## Santiago Atitian, Guatemala - February 1964

The first bombers came in low and fast, bombs falling from their silver bellies, and were gone. Next came explosions, followed by shock waves and flying material that had once been the market. Something hit Maria in the chest and knocked her to the ground. Instinctively, she rolled to her knees and crawled under a nearby table. The next bombers followed the routes of the first wave, but when their bombs exploded, the explosions were more muffled and up sprang swirling black clouds containing roiling orange fire.

Battlefield accounts from soldiers relate a strange effect from a nearby bomb blast. They speak of all their senses – except vision - shutting down for a period of time. There are no sounds, smells, or feelings of any sort. There are no emotions or thoughts. It is as if all human sensors have been overwhelmed and simply stopped working.

That was most certainly the case for Maria, who hugged the ground and peered out from her shelter. Flaming building debris was floating down from the sky like surreal autumn leaves. Nearby, a woman lay on her back, her opens eyes gazing skyward. Blood was flowing from her mouth. Fruit and nuts and loaves of bread and brightly colored clothing with coded embroideries from the tables and racks, were scattered everywhere.

Maria blinked and stared.

Then came the fires. At first, there was just smoke, but soon, bright yellow flames began shooting skyward with a roar. She crawled out from under the table and sat in the middle of the street. Wherever she looked, buildings were ablaze. Black smoke was filling the sky.

She knew she had to leave, but her body was numb and unwilling.

Maria just blinked and stared.

Her ears were ringing, her limbs were unresponsive. Heavy. Lying on her lap like a rag doll.

The next thing she knew, a man was pulling her to her feet. He was yelling something in K'iche' but Maria couldn't understand. Then he shouted "DEBOMOS SALIR DE AQUI!" and that she knew.

"We must leave?" she asked drunkenly, as if coming out of a fog. "Why? What has happened?"

Ignoring her question, he put his arm around her shoulder and half led, half dragged her off the street, down the trail to the lake, to the water's edge.

His face was smeared with soot and he smelled of sweat, and something else. It was fear. That was it, fear.

Once at the lake, many other villagers were taking to the old dugout canoes. Babies were crying, dogs were barking. The man who smelled of fear lowered Maria into the bow of a larger vessel with two other women – one bleeding profusely from her right ear - and shouted to the man in the back, "LEJOS!" The man in the stern jumped out, shoved Maria's canoe away from shore, jumped back aboard, and began vigorously paddling.

He skillfully steered the boat along the shore, staying hidden from the town above by keeping close to the dense mangrove thickets. They were fleeing from the hell fires up on the hill. Where they were going was not important as long as it was away. Far away.

Now a new sound punctuated the air: Trucks, many trucks, approaching from the east. Then tailgates banged open and the sound of men's voices could be heard. They were shouting orders. Then came staccato gun fire. More shouts. More orders. Then screams. Then more gun fire.

Maria gazed at the woman behind her. The bleeding had subsided, but her face was now the color of thinned milk. Her eyes were no longer blinking, and her head had slouched to the left.

The other woman was sobbing into her hands and slowly rocking forward and back, forward and back.

Maria lay down and rested her head on the bow of the boat, watching the water smoothly slide by. She remembered the night she paddled across the lake when the moonlight slid down the side of the volcano and danced across the water.

Surely, that was a lifetime ago.

*Sue's Comments: I had been to Guatemala and learned a bit of the recent history of those resilient people. Choosing that topic for my historical fiction was a natural for me, but I think I gave my fellow HPs (Hot Potatoes), who didn't have the same connection to the place and people that I did, a real challenge. As usual, they rose to it beautifully.*

*Donna's Comments: Again, research saved me from a total washout on this one. Sue set up a factual scenario, and I clearly struggled to maintain some semblance of story line. On my part, too much imagination and not enough fact for this genre. Alan saved the day.*

*Alan's Comments: When I first read the story written*

*by Sue and then augmented by Donna, I thought about calling them and asking to write something else. I knew nothing about this entire sad story and in fact am not sure if I could find Guatemala on a map. But like Donna says, research and Wikipedia can save the day. A departure from our usual but a worthy exercise.*

# THE MEETING

By Alan, Donna, Sue

It was hot, Colorado style. I sat on a log which mercifully, was bathed in dappled sunshine, care of an enormous cottonwood tree. The Dolores River flowed merrily by, on its way to wherever rivers go. Fishing was slow but no matter – it was my idea of relaxing.

Life was just about perfect. Not a care. But all that changed in quite literally, the blink of an eye. One moment I was alone on my log, the next moment, a man was seated beside me.

With a jolt, I stared at the intruder. It was as if looking in a mirror. It was me seated beside me.

He returned my gaze and smiled. "Hello Alan."

"Who..." I began.

"Oh, I think you already know," he replied. "I, of course, am you. I live in a parallel universe and thought it might be nice to drop by and pay you a visit." He glanced at some sort of wristwatch. "And by the way, we have just 13 minutes."

"Wha..." I stammered.

"It's just like the story you wrote. *Wormhole.* Remember?"

"How did you..."

"A portal."

I blinked a few times. "Really? But my story was science fiction."

He smiled again. "Well, surprise! You nailed it."

I pursed my lips. *Have I fallen asleep? This dream seems to be real.* I reached down to the river, cupped a handful of water, then splashed my face.

I looked and the guy was still there.

"Eleven minutes," he said. "We're down to eleven minutes." He crossed his legs and took in the scenery. "Nice spot. I can see why you're here." After a moment, he turned toward me and said, "Here's what happened: universes float around like bubbles on a river, just flowing through a dimension neither you nor I can understand. Once in a while, the flow becomes turbulent, just like the rapids out there in the river. When that happens, the universes can be tossed together, and when *that* happens, a portal between them opens. Follow?"

"Who are you really?" I asked.

"Eight minutes. That's how long before the portal closes. When that happens, I'm gone. Follow?"

I took out my pipe and packed it with Virginia Burley tobacco, all the while staring at the intruder.

I struck a match. "So," puff, puff, "What's this all about?" puff, puff.

"I don't have the time to go into too much detail, but I just wanted to stop by and tell you something big is about to happen."

I tossed the wooden match into the river and watched it float away. "Something big? If we are in parallel universes, how would you know?"

The guy checked his watch again. "You already

know the answer to that. It's in your story. We're fifty years ahead of you guys. And I know your immediate future. Five minutes by the way."

"I see. So, what's this big event? Is an asteroid coming our way?"

"Nope. This is something that will make you incredibly happy."

"Does it have anything to do with the presidential election?"

"No. It's personal."

I puffed on my pipe. "So, are you going to tell me or is this some kind of elaborate guessing game?"

The guy stood and looked at his watch again. "You don't seem very excited."

"Well, you know, I'm still not sure about you. There's something fishy about this, this..." I waved my pipe at him, "this all of a sudden, dropped out of the sky, meeting. It isn't every day I meet someone who claims to be me from another dimension."

"Not *another dimension*, a *parallel universe!*"

"Whatever."

He waded a few steps into the river. "A modicum of gratitude might be in order here. My journey wasn't exactly a walk in the park." He checked his watch again. "Adios my friend."

Then he was gone.

Just as my doppelganger faded into the thin Colorado air, two Broad-tailed hummingbirds appeared, dancing and hovering over the ripples he left behind. As always, their happiness mesmerized me into total relaxation, and I sat back down to watch the free show. The Dolores caught their reflection with the wet ones shimmering from reality of the two above.

I shook myself back to my own reality. "O.K., since that did not just happen, what did it mean? I need to analyze this. My other self, still handsome from fifty years in the future, just delivered some 'incredibly happy' news about my immediate future. That's what he...I...told myself. And it has to do with *Wormhole*, the novella I published in my short story collection."

The hummers flitted away, apparently annoyed that they had lost my full attention. I relit my pipe and puffed again, savoring the tobacco's soft, nutty flavor. Smooth. Slow burn. My anxiety waned.

"That's it! Patience is a virtue that I rarely appreciate. My happy news is that my multiple attempts to have *Wormhole* accepted as a mini-series have finally paid off!" There was only one problem with my need to scramble back to the house to get the mail or listen to my answering machine or hear Ann give me the good news. I could not move.

Two horseflies landed on the hand that held my pipe, but I could only stare down at them. Couldn't flick them off or blow them away or shoo them back to wherever they came from. My skin ruffled, but the iridescent duo just walked along the pipe stem, mocking my inability to make them leave me alone.

I'm having a stroke, I told myself. Just as I'm about to learn that *Netflix* has picked up my story, I'm having a fricking stroke. My mirror image tried to warn me, tried to remind me to be patient, but now it was too late. The river flowed three feet from where I sat, frozen in time. It seemed to take hours for my eyes to change focus from the river to my feet, where I panicked at the sight of my untied shoes. Sweat began to stream from under my hat, into my moustache and onto my shirt, darkening from light khaki to a muddy grayish brown.

As the sun began to set, my body seemed to lighten, as if I were hovering over myself. Still, I could not move. The horseflies had done what I wanted. They left me alone. I was alone with my thoughts, my big dreams and missed opportunities. The realization came to me then. If I had jumped up to run back to the house, I would have tripped on my untied shoelaces and fallen into the river, never to have enjoyed the fruits of my labor.

Gradually, with infinitesimal slowness, like the lesson of the Beach Sand Corollary, I painstakingly tied each shoelace, double-knotted them and pulled myself up to a stand on the shore. The lesson here is to savor the moment, and I was grateful for the turbulence that caused a slight collision of my parallel universe.

Now, I tell you reader, I turned expecting to see the familiar path and my Land Rover, waiting in the darkness. I hope you will believe what I saw instead.

There before me, half-hidden in a glowing haze, was an object that looked as if it had fallen off the pages of an old comic book – a spaceship of the upside-down cup and saucer variety. I half expected to see little green Martians running around. Today was turning out to be beyond my wildest imaginings. Even my sci-fi stories were better grounded than this.

"Aaah, Alan. I've been waiting for you. It took you long enough," said a familiar voice from inside the spaceship.

"Wait a minute! I thought you were in a big hurry to get back to your dimension."

"Universe, Alan. Parallel universe. I was testing you. As I said, *patience*. An answer, please?"

"I was tying my frigging shoelaces. If you're so damn smart, you ought to know that." My calm mood of just moments ago had evaporated and I was becoming increasingly annoyed at the smug self-assurance of my double. *Wait,* I checked myself, *is that what I look like when I think I've scored one? Hmm. Better watch out.*

He laughed heartily. "I thought that since I had come all this way, we could take a few minutes to get to know each other." He sat down on the edge of the saucer part of the ship and patted the space beside him for me to sit, but I nodded, indicating that I preferred to stand. "We live in a parallel universe and look identical, but that doesn't mean that we have parallel lives. I must say that I rather like this fishing gig you have – I'll give it a go when I get back. And the pipe. Nice touch. Much more suave than a cigar."

I have to admit that I was getting a little curious. "And I assume you read, since you know about *Wormhole*."

"Of course - and I've read all the other stories in *Innkeeper* and *Reboot* as well. But since we are so much ahead of you technologically, I don't have to take the time to actually *read* them – I must admit *Wormhole* was a bit long for a short story . . ."

"Novella. It's a novella. It's supposed to be long."

"Whatever, I was going to say it was a good length for a miniseries. Anyway, we just teledigest by staring at the copy for a few minutes and *bingo*, we've absorbed everything. Quite efficient, actually."

I was having a hard time – I felt like I was split in two. Part of me – the writer part that loved imagining alternate worlds and characters – was intrigued by this being and his story. The other part – the rational engineer who just wanted to get back home, check in with Ann, and have a stiff drink and dinner – was chafing under his commanding presence. But I did have a question I wanted to ask. "So, do you like to write stories too?"

"But of course," he laughed. "That's how I got here."

"What??!" This was pushing the envelope.

"You know how here, when you write a story, like *Wormhole*, say, a company like *Netflix* might make it into a series, act it out, make it *seem* real?"

"Yeah, yeah go on." He had my attention now – *Wormhole* .... *Netflix*. Was he hinting? Was this the good thing that was going to happen?

"Well, in our universe, we skip all that in between stuff and just create reality, so we *live* our stories. Certain genres, like murder mysteries and war stories, are outlawed. As you can imagine, Romance is a big seller. But anyway, I got the idea of writing about slipping through a wormhole and visiting you from your story, and here I am. However, we do have our limits, and I am going to have to get back shortly." He stood up to let me know our time was at an end.

"Wait! Before you go – two questions. First, about this 'something big' that's going to happen. Would it by any chance have anything to do with this very story we have been talking about?"

"Oh, Alan. I told you I'm not at liberty to reveal details, but I can tell you that in a short time some of your writing will be presented to a very appreciative audience. Question two?"

"If you came through a wormhole, what's with this kitschy flying saucer?"

He laughed again. He – I? – did have a cheerful laugh. "This is just a holograph. It will disappear when I take my leave, which is now."

And in the blink of an eye, without a fare-thee-well, he and the spaceship were gone and in their place was my Land Rover.

I couldn't wait to get back to Ann and get a reality check. Was I still all here? Had I been changed by my encounter? And I particularly wanted to tell her about the special thing that was going to happen. Could it be . . .? He certainly hinted enough. It had to be – *Netflix* was going to pick up *Wormhole*. I was sure.

I pulled into the driveway, hastily parked the car, and ran into the house.

"There you are!" Ann greeted me. "Where have you been? Never mind, come on into the den. Someone's waiting for you."

I was right! Someone from *Netflix* wanting to discuss their upcoming miniseries. My double had hit it on the nose.

"They want you to read your latest piece."

There, on my computer screen, were Donna and Sue waiting for me to begin.

*Alan's Comments: I have written – but not yet published - a trilogy entitled Wormhole and this story is a*

*shameless advertisement for my future best seller. As always, I was amused and bemused at the contributions from Donna and Sue. They are full of surprises. What a treat to have pals like them!*

*Donna's Comments: Alan introduced this Sc-Fi piece and I couldn't resist taunting him with references to his own words. Sue picked it up and ran with it.*

*Sue's Comments: This one was fun to write, playing with a lot of "in jokes" about Alan's novella Wormhole, which we would all love to see made into a Netflix miniseries.*

# TRAVELOGUE

### By Sue, Alan, Donna

"**A**re we almost there yet?" Grogan murmured through the haze of the Comadose-induced sleep necessary to take her through the long journey. This was only the fifth intergalactic cruise to have left Herta, and it had required a hefty outlay of pergins. But Grogan and her husband, along with the other two couples onboard, had felt it worth the expense for the status it assured them. They would be the envy of the whole country, and what stories they would have to tell!

She poked her husband, who was immersed in a following a hydro-spacial transmittal of the final championship game of nungen, the national sport of Herta. "Cluren, I'm talking to you."

"Hum?" he said, opening one of his ears to her, but keeping the others intensely focused on the game. He had been very annoyed that the trip was scheduled during the final games and indeed had tried to use his extensive influence to change the date, but to no avail. He was told kindly but firmly that the extraordinary preparations for this momentous journey took precedence over a game, even an interplanetary championship.

"Shouldn't we be getting near Taypah, or Tappa, or

whatever's the name of that planet the travel agent told us we would be going to?"

"Yeah, probably. Ask that dumb midian who is supposed to be taking care of us," he mumbled and turned his full attention back to the game.

Grogan nodded her head at the summoner beam, and the attendant appeared before her. She was dressed in a tan uniform, her hefty tan arms and broad tan face only a slightly lighter shade, and she seemed to blend into the background, something midians were long accustomed to doing. "Yes ma'am. What can I do for you?" she asked.

"When are we going to be in Taypah?" There was an edge to Grogon's voice; after all, she had been rendered immobile for an unendurably long time, though in fact it was not terribly far from her normal state.

The attendant hesitated. "I'm afraid there has been a slight change in plans. We're in the right galaxy, but somehow we have ended up in the wrong solar system. Our new destination is Earth, which I have been assured you will find much to your liking. I understand you will have an opportunity to view creatures in a primitive stage of development, and the accommodations should be more or less comfortable."

Cluren perked up all his ears to take in this new bit of information. "What the frog do you mean, 'We're in the wrong solar system'? This is unacceptable!"

"Watch your language, please, Cluren," Grogan sputtered.

"Language smanguage! Send me that blinging widdan who is supposed to be in control of this ship." Cluren had no patience for anyone who performed less than perfectly, especially if it was a lowly widdan.

Cluren blinked several times as he looked at the being who now stood before him. Like all widdans, the captain's skin was pasty white, the inevitable outcome of endless generations living beyond where the faint rays of the sun ever reached. It lacked the rich deep luster of fristons like Cluren and Grogan, who owned the mesas, close to the sun. There they were able to spread out their great expanse of skin to absorb those precious rays, becoming a deep, dark, luxuriant black. Since it was only on the mesas that roncle, the succulent that all Hertans needed to survive, sprouted freely, and the fristons controlled the mesas, they effectively controlled the planet. Although over the generations the widdons had developed the technology that kept everything moving forward, their total dependence on the fristons for sustenance had reduced them to a subservient class. Even the midians, who lived perched on the sides of the mesas and survived as the middlemen between the other two groups, were deemed less menial.

No, it wasn't the slenderness or the pale hair or the white skin that surprised Cluren; he was certainly accustomed to that. It was the fact that the captain was a woman.

"What the . . ." he looked at his wife's disapproving glare and held his tongue. "A woman!! No wonder we're lost." He turned to the other two couples comfortably ensconced in the capsule. "Do you believe they put a woman in charge? I don't believe these widdans! And of course, she gets us lost! I say we make sure we get a big refund when we get back."

"Shut up Idiot," said the man in the closest seat. Cluren was not exactly a favorite of the group. "You seem to have forgotten that we don't *get* back unless *she* takes us. So sit down, close your mouth, and make nice. Let's just hope she can forget everything you've said."

After a heated and tense conversation with the captain, wherein Cluren and Grogan insisted on sticking with their original plans to visit Taypah, it was grudgingly agreed to stick with the itinerary. This would require a brief layover – no more than 24 hours – at an orbiting service station near Earth for refueling and recalibration.

Hubby Cluren and the other couples decided to remain onboard and slip back into a drug related sleep (with the help of another hit of Comadose) but Grogan would not hear of it. Instead, she decided to use the down time to do a little exploring.

First, she changed into a human form. Then, armed with a wad of the local currency, a translator's handbook, and a GPS system for navigation, Grogan beamed down to a place known as Fenway Park, aka home of the Boston Red Sox. It quickly became apparent that a large crowd of natives had gathered, about to enter some sort of large coliseum.

Grogan had been taught that the first order of the inter-galactic travel business was to blend with the natives. She looked around. All the earthlings wore a blue hat with a red B emblazoned of the front, carried in one hand an enormous foam finger with RED SOX printed upon it, and in the other, a magazine of some sort.

Nearby, a portly man, standing behind a kiosk counter, was yelling, "PROGRAMS. GET YOUR PROGRAMS!" She approached him.

"Excuse me," she said. "I'd like to buy one of those

(she pointed at a Red Sox hat), one of those (she pointed at a foam finger), and one of those magazines" (she pointed at the program.)

"TWENTY-FIVE," he shouted.

"Twenty-five what?" she asked.

"Bucks."

She withdrew the handful of cash. "Which of these..."

He took a five and a twenty, tossed them into an open cigar box, passed her the merchandise, then resumed yelling, "PROGRAMS. GET YOUR PROGRAMS!"

The doors to the coliseum opened and the crowd surged forward, sweeping Grogan along.

The next stop occurred when some guy with a yellow vest held out his hand and said, "Ticket."

"Ticket?"

"Yeah. I need your ticket."

"What does it look like?"

"Hit the road lady. Next."

Grogan was jostled out of the way. She no sooner had time to collect her thoughts when another guy, standing in the shadows, emerged and said, "Hey lady. Need a ticket?"

"Well, apparently so."

"Fifty bucks. Box seat. First base line."

Grogan began to reach for her translator, but the guy seemed to be impatient. "Fifty bucks. Take it or leave it."

She again withdrew her wad of cash and held it out. The guy took four fifty-dollar bills, handed over something that could only be a ticket, and dashed away into the shadows.

A moment later, she was back in the que. The ticket guy took her ticket, ripped it in half (handing her back one piece) and said, "Straight ahead, up the stairs, third row on the left." Then he looked past her to the next person in line. "Ticket?"

Following the curt instructions, she went straight ahead, up the stairs, then took the third row on the left.

A man, wearing a yellow vest with the word USHER stenciled across the front, held out his hand.

Grogan looked at him.

He said, "Lemmie see your ticket."

She did.

He pointed. "On the end, two rows down."

She did as directed, taking her seat. Grogan had just started to take in the sights, when two women showed up. They wore Boston Red Sox shirts, the requisite blue hat with a red B, and both carried programs.

"Excuse us," the first one said with a smile.

They took the next two seats in, and immediately began an endless stream of chatter. It must have had something to do with the fellows on the big green lawn because they kept pointing and checking their programs.

Finally, the woman next to Grogan looked her way. "Hi," she said. "I'm Donna. This is Sue," she nodded towards her companion. "Are you an Indians fan?"

Grogan shook her head. "I don't think so."

"Just checking," Donna said. "Normally, that seat is taken by someone from the away team. What's your name?"

"I'm Grogan. And I have to tell you, I'm new to all of this. What's about to happen out there?"

For the next ten minutes, Donna and Sue talked non-stop about pitchers, infielders, batting averages, pennant races, and something called base stealing. Grogan didn't understand a word of it.

Then, some guy was making his way down the stairs with a big box slung over his shoulder. "HOT DOGS, BEER, POPCORN, CRACKER JACKS!" he yelled.

Sue raised her hand, and said to Grogan, "My treat." Then to the vendor, she said, "Three dogs, three beers."

They settled back in their seats and prepared to get to it. Grogan watched them and tried to copy what they did.

First was a healthy gulp of the bubbly yellow liquid. Grogan gagged and wanted to spit it out. It was bitter and lacking any flavor that could be called pleasant. But she swallowed and tried to smile.

Next came the thing in the wrapper. *What did she call it? A dog?* Grogan got out her translator and looked up dog: *Domestic four-legged animal.*

She unwrapped the package and stared at the thing in the bread bun.

"Excuse me," she said to Donna. "What part of the dog did you get?"

Then a booming voice said, "ALL RISE FOR THE SINGING OF THE NATION ANTHEM."

As Donna and Sue stood, Grogan put down her dog, and slipped away.

Grogan had had enough of that nonsense. Watching that Boston Red Sox thing was little better than listening to Cluren's obsession with nungen. But it was better. At least these primitive Earth creatures exhibited some personal interaction and actually sat in the same atmosphere as the game being played. All nungen fans could do was listen to the competition via stereo ears. And those women, Donna and Sue, seemed to think she, Grogan, was one of them. They even had the audacity to buy a very black stranger some food, as if the stranger weren't above them.

No one noticed or cared that Grogan left the place called Fenway Park, contrary to the difficult time she had getting in. She watched as a few stragglers filtered through with tickets and hats and fingers and programs, not noticing her departure at all. And so many skin colors all meshed together. That tan-skinned midian Donna and her ghostly-white widdan friend Sue showed no reserved respect for Grogan. She puzzled at their companionship and walked quickly away from the loud mass of humanity behind her.

"I have many hours left in this layover," she told herself, "and I'm going to make the most of it. What else can I explore?"

The tall ebony Hertan tossed hat, program and finger in a nearby can, since few of the Earthlings along her walk were similarly encumbered. Her transposed human form, dressed in faded jeans and a t-shirt, drew no attention. Grogan paused to tap in coordinates on her GPS, set the transporter for twenty hours, and walked on, curious to see what else this primitive species did to pass the time.

A line of them stood waiting to get into something called Skywalk Observatory. Smirking at their backward desire to "see 360-degree views of Boston and beyond," Grogan pressed TRANSPORT on her armband, thought of being on the top, and opened her eyes to a city of lights. No one noticed her sudden appearance, but she noticed the multicolored, multilingual mass marveling at the view. This is unique, she thought.

Next stop, a Hop-on, Hop-off Trolley Tour, requiring some more of her bucks. The Isabella Stewart Gardner Museum attracted these strangers from all over the world, yet here what she came to understand was the USA part of Earth, people flocked to see European, American and Asian art in the replica of a Venetian palace. "So confusing, such a mixture of cultures here," Grogan puzzled.

From the trolley, she observed the Freedom Trail, a Bunker Hill Monument, a symphony hall, and a monument erected to honor war dead. Grogan could not fathom why people seemed to cherish the past and marvel at the history of a primitive people. She could hear languages from around the rest of the world and wondered why they were here.

When she stepped off the trolley, Grogan smelled roncle and hoped she could find something better than dog parts on bread. She read out loud, "Pizza and Cannoli," and an Asian man returned most of the bucks she handed him.

Three young people, one black, one yellow and one white, pulled her aside and suggested she not flash so much money around on the street. She nodded, confused at their kindness. "Get a debit card," the young girl whispered.

"So much for impressing the Hertans with my intergalactic cruise. So much for establishing status among the less elite back home. This is a most wonderful place."

She reset her transporter for twenty years and took a bite of this thing they called pizza.

*Sue's Comments: When I passed this on to Alan, I certainly never expected my main character to end up in Fenway Park. Or wandering through Boston. One of the main things this whole experiment has revealed to me is that a story can have many wonderful lives if you are just willing to let your imagination run free.*

*Alan's Comments: No space traveler or alien drifter could ever stop by without taking in a game at Fenway park. And you know, I believe I sat next to some of them at some of the games I attended. One time, a fellow seated next to me drank eight beers by the 5th inning then left, never to be seen again. I'm sure he was from some distant galaxy. Also, Donna's implication that pizza was cause for time travel is right on target!*

*Donna's comments: The challenge here is that I had neither been an intergalactic alien nor had I ever been to Fenway Park. But, I love baseball, did a little research on the local color, and finished the story far, far away from where it began.*

# BAGGAGE

By Donna, Sue, Alan

And away we went. Turn back to the beginning and enjoy!

**The End**

# THANK YOU!

We have been blessed with readers who were willing to take out a red pen and edit, correct, suggest, and most importantly, offer encouragement to continue writing our manuscript. Thank you, a million times! Thank you.

The readers are:

Mary Weaver
Marcy Abbott
Ann Mulak
Susan McCool
Michelle Mulak
Vicki Forsht Williams
Donna Kaminski
Roz McCarthy
Bill McCarthy
Robin Pascucci
Mary Ann Hume

# QUESTIONS
# FOR BOOK CLUB READERS

1. Thomas' life gradually improved after each mysterious transport. Which people most influenced him to shed his baggage? How?

2. How did working in a bookstore make Thomas' unlikely travels more credible?

3. If Thomas had never found the suitcases, would Cherie have given him a second look?

4. What do you think of the character of Thomas? Did your feelings about him change throughout the story?

5. Which adventure did you enjoy the most? Why?

6. Of the fourteen other stories we three writers created before *Baggage* evolved, are there any others which could have been stretched further?

7. Just for fun, re-read the beginning of one of the stories and pretend it was handed to you. Where would you have gone with the story? Or stop before

the end and finish it up. Did that give you any in-sight into what fun the three authors must have had writing these stories?

8. Which of the short stories do you think was the most successful? Which was the least?

9. If you had a chance to touch the suitcases and travel anywhere you wanted, when and where would you go?

CPSIA information can be obtained
at www.ICGtesting.com
Printed in the USA
LVHW111309250621
691139LV00003B/193